Dedalus Original Fiction in Paperback

Robert Irwin (born in 1946) is a novelist, historian, critic and scholar. He is a fellow of The Royal Society of Literature.

Robert is the author of ten novels: *The Arabian Nightmare* (1983), *The Limits of Vision* (1986), *The Mysteries of Algiers* (1988), *Exquisite Corpse* (1995), *Prayer-Cushions of the Flesh* (1997), *Satan Wants Me* (1999) *Wonders Will Never Cease* (2016), *My Life is Like a Fairy Tale* (2019), *The Runes Have Been Cast* (2021) and *Tom's Version* (2023).

All Robert's novels have enjoyed substantial publicity and commercial success although he is best known for *The Arabian Nightmare* which has been translated into twenty languages and is considered by many critics to be one of the great literary fantasy novels of the twentieth century.

Robert Irwin

TOM'S VERSION

Dedalus

Supported using public funding by
**ARTS COUNCIL
ENGLAND**

Published in the UK by Dedalus Limited
24-26, St Judith's Lane, Sawtry, Cambs, PE28 5XE
info@dedalusbooks.com
www.dedalusbooks.com

ISBN printed book 978 1 915568 27 4
ISBN ebook 978 1 915568 44 1

Dedalus is distributed in the USA & Canada by SCB Distributors
15608 South New Century Drive, Gardena, CA 90248
info@scbdistributors.com   www.scbdistributors.com

Dedalus is distributed in Australia by Peribo Pty Ltd
58, Beaumont Road, Mount Kuring-gai, N.S.W. 2080
info@peribo.com.au   www.peribo.com.au

First published by Dedalus in 2023
Tom's Version copyright © Robert Irwin 2023

Printed and bound in the UK by Clays Elcograf S.p A.
Typeset by Marie Lane

A C.I.P. listing for this book is available on request.

all the people in this novel are, unfortunately, fictional, except of course for Philip IV of France, Robert Louis Stevenson, J. R. R. Tolkien and Tom Byrne

CHAPTER ONE

October, 1970

Their clothes were piled around the edges of the room. It had taken Philip nearly twenty minutes to persuade them that they needed to be naked before they started. Clothes were just another form of armour that would conceal their real personalities not only from other people but also from themselves. Not that he was ordering them to strip. He was only their guide and he was there to take the group wherever the group wanted to go. The rather nice-looking young Scottish woman protested at length that she did not want all these men ogling 'ma manky body'. But Philip had his way and now he was proposing that each of them in turn should stand up, give their Christian name and then in a sentence or two say something about why they were here or make a statement that defined who they were, or both. He was only proposing, mind, not instructing, and, if the group wanted to do something else, that was fine by him.

There were twelve of them, six men and six women, plus Philip. And they were mostly young, middle class and all white. They lounged awkwardly on cushions arranged in a circle. The basement had no windows, its floor-level lighting gave their faces a cadaverous look and the smell of burning joss sticks suggested that some strange ritual was about to begin. Several of the women looked attractive. Even so, the set-up did not seem very promising to Tom. His companions looked hesitantly at one another, until finally the man whose demeanour and discarded clothes had suggested that he was some kind of businessman rose to his feet.

'I am Raymond,' he said and then he added, 'I am so lonely.'

Philip nodded and indicated that it was the turn of the jolly middle-aged woman sitting next to Raymond.

'Hi, I'm Melanie and I'm a hundred-per-cent pro-life.'

'I'm Jeff and I thought this might be a bit of a laugh and you're not going to tell me that I am wrong… here we all are sitting starkers.'

'Sally is my name and I want to find my way to the Golden Land that I have glimpsed in my dreams.'

Then, 'I am Leon. I have cancer and I want to learn how to die well.'

That was weird and he was so young! But what followed was weirder yet, when a statuesque and beautiful young woman rose to speak, 'My name is Molly and I am accursed, for I bring bad luck, fucking bad luck, to every man I sleep with.'

This was so very weird that Tom missed the names and statements of the next three participants. Perhaps this Molly person was using the I-am-accursed spiel as a kind of chastity belt? Or, more likely, she was just nuts.

Then it was his turn, 'Hi, I'm Tom. I am here to achieve my inner potential and find in others a mirror of my hopes and ideals.'

A load of old cobblers of course. He had picked up this sort of feel-good garbage from the literature put out for encounter groups by Esalen and Quaesitor. Some of this group looked impressed, though Philip was looking at him suspiciously. So Tom was lying, but so what? He did not believe that any of those he had heard had spoken the truth about themselves.

Then Philip wanted every participant in succession to turn to the person on their left, and on the basis of that person's appearance and the statement that he or she had just made, they should act out their impression of that person. This was awkward for Tom since, distracted by Molly's self-denunciation, he missed the name and statement of his neighbour. Though this was a bit embarrassing, it was soon sorted out. Ferdie was on drugs and he loved the drug experience, but now he wanted to find a straight way of achieving a high. Apart from anything else, it might be cheaper. Tom thought that this was not entirely true and that Ferdie probably had more serious problems. But he did his best with what Ferdie had given him. The man's thick black hair which stuck out in triangles on either side of his head gave him the appearance of a clown. His teeth were awful and there was a hint of bad breath. As for Ferdie's take on Tom, Tom was Mister Super-Cool.

Meanwhile, a row had broken out elsewhere in the circle. Sally had refused to believe that Leon really had cancer and he was slapping her face and weeping with rage as he did so. So Philip strode over and separated them. Then he went out of the room and came back with two swords and instructed them, no, advised them, to fight it out in the middle of the circle. This was so very daft. The blades of the swords were of foam rubber. But Tom, watching the fight, thought that he might be able to use this for what he had in mind, only the swords would have to have blades of steel. After ten minutes of this nonsense, it was the turn of Sally to start weeping. Perhaps some kind of catharsis had been achieved. No, not quite, for she could not stop weeping. So Philip advised the rest of the group to gather round Sally, lift her off the ground and rock her gently in their arms. She was safe and part of a group, all of whom loved her.

And so it continued. Each person had to act out one of their parents. One by one they had to dance to the music that was in their head. Towards the end there was a meditation. Finally Philip announced that he was going to pair them up for co-counselling and in the coming fortnight, sometime before the next Quaesitor session, they should arrange to meet and try to work as their opposite number's guide or therapist. Co-counselling is not the same as having a chat. They should take turns to be the counsellor who would listen at length and with full attention to whatever their companion who was their client wanted to say. The client had to be absolutely free to say whatever he or she wished, and whatever was said should remain totally confidential. Then, when the fortnight was up, they should all report briefly to the group on how the co-counselling had gone, without revealing any personal confidences. Tom was assigned Melanie, a cheery middle-aged woman, but when they had made their way up to the ground floor, they were stopped in the hall by Raymond and Molly.

'Sorry to bother you,' said Raymond, 'but we don't feel we would be very suited to one another. Would you mind dreadfully if we swapped and you co-counselled Molly, while

I took Melanie off your hands?'

Tom had no objection to swapping Melanie for a younger model, but what he said was, 'Philip won't like it. He decided who should go with who.'

'But Philip is not in charge is he? He said that he wasn't and that we are not here to live up to his expectations.'

Molly smiled. It was the smile of a glamorous woman. Tom threw up his hands. And so it was agreed. Raymond and Melanie went off together.

Turning to Tom, Molly said, 'Thank God, not Raymond. I did not want to be the answer to his lonely hearts column ad.'

'When? And your place or mine?'

'I think it should be on neutral ground don't you?'

Tom proposed a weekend meeting, but she was not free then. It would have to be a weekday lunchtime. Cranks Vegetarian Restaurant in Marshall Street was reasonably close to where she worked. Thursday after next. They walked in silence to St John's Wood Underground Station, but at this point Tom decided that he was not in the mood that evening to spend more time with this difficult woman and that he was going to walk on down the hill to Chalk Farm Station.

London was so full of stories. The moon, one of Yeats' 'silver apples', was riding high over the clouds. This encounter business seemed to promise well for him. It would be so easy to satirise, but then the satire should deepen into tragedy. Maybe that madwoman would turn out to be good material. A new life, a new career might be about to begin. He was still young and the road of life stretched endlessly ahead. Somewhere on that road Maeve was surely waiting for him. He was Tom in the City of Adventures.

CHAPTER TWO

Though it had not been easy for Tom to take time off, on the specified Thursday he made his way to Cranks. He was early and he would have liked a proper drink, but there was nothing on offer except dodgy-looking fruit-and-vegetable-juices. The seats were uncomfortable and the food on offer looked horribly healthy. Molly arrived a few minutes later. He had not noticed what she was wearing at the encounter group. Then, of course, most of the time she had been wearing nothing. But now, as she made her entrance, heads turned. She was wearing a broad-brimmed floppy scarlet hat, a red embroidered waistcoat over a white blouse and a black maxi skirt. Though she was certainly beautiful, Tom judged that she might have been born too late and that her beauty belonged to a past age. Her style, her luxuriant hair and slightly florid features suggested a *grande dame* of the nineteenth-century stage. She was beautiful, but not, he thought, as Maeve was beautiful. Molly scanned the room carefully before joining him at his table.

They shook hands before going to the counter and they both collected mixed vegetable soup with a salad and a wholemeal roll on their trays. The salad had a lot of odd-looking red seeds in it and they had to ask, what they were. 'Quinoa.' The answer left them none the wiser, but with the quinoa problem unresolved, they cautiously began the conversation that should turn into a co-counselling session.

'That blonde hair, that tan, that moustache — until you opened your mouth I'd guessed you were American, maybe Californian,' she said. 'You're a surfer dude who just needed dark glasses to complete the outfit.'

'Well, no. I come from a small village in the south of Ireland.'

'What do you do for a living, Tom?'

'I supervise a warehouse in Nine Elms in south-east London,' he said and enjoyed the look of disappointment on her face. 'And you?'

'I was born in Guildford. I am with the sales department at Sotheby's auction house. I used to sit at the reception desk, give directions, sell catalogues and stuff like that, but now they use me to greet prospective high-rolling bidders. Also they get me to pose for press photographers. I hold up a Flemish miniature or a Japanese vase and I have to look at it lovingly, as if I could imagine no greater happiness than to possess such an object.'

For both of them that meeting last week had been their first experience of an encounter group. What an oddly assembled gang of people, needy folk, perhaps the discards of society. They both agreed that Philip had seemed very nervous. It was probably his first time at being group leader and the slightest challenge to his authority seemed to worry him. As for the group exercises, it was a bit like being at primary school again, though there was also the unpleasant undercurrent of an adult truth game. What is the worst thing you have ever done? When did you last cry? Whom would you most like to kiss in this room? Sooner or later, if they kept turning up to that basement in St John's Wood, these and similar questions would come up. One would have to be a real masochist to want to attend these sessions — The St John's Wood Masochists Anonymous. It was easy for the two of them to agree on all this, but it was not co-counselling. So eventually Tom asked, 'What was all that stuff about you being accursed and a hazard to all men?'

'Oh no, you first. Why did you leave Ireland and have you found fulfilment as a warehouse manager, or is it just possible that there's something a teeny-weeny bit more exciting that you are ready for and that is why you have signed up for the group?'

How to reply? How much truth did this woman deserve?

'I come from the village of Cashel in County Tipperary. It is, as I have said, in the south. As a boy, I played in the shadow of the medieval ruins of Cashel Mount. When childhood was over, I left the village to study law in Dublin. But the law did not suit me and besides Maeve remained in Cashel. It was Maeve who had introduced me to the poetry of W. B. Yeats and I am not sure that she did me any favours by that, for the poetry is now like a fever in my blood. "Irish poets learn your trade, Sing whatever is well made…" We were standing on the slope of Cashel Mount in a high wind and we were both shouting. I shouted that I had decided to become a poet. She laughed in my face and she told me that, now that I had failed at law, my best chance was to find employment as the local butcher's boy. I remember her long red hair blowing across her face as she spoke and that she looked like a Celtic prophetess

14

who was speaking from behind a veil. I told her that I would not return to Cashel except as a successful poet. Then she should kneel before me on this hillside and confess her error. I did not look back as I walked down to the village. Then I crossed over to England to prove myself…'

Molly interrupted, 'Fine words! Or, to look at it another way, gobshite! And you are not a successful poet are you? And what are you? Thirty?'

'Almost.'

Molly was relentless, 'But perhaps Maeve will be impressed, if she follows you over to England and finds you installed with your packing cases in your warehouse in southeast London.'

Tom hesitated, before continuing, 'I suppose I do deserve your mockery. Yet I find that the warehouse is a blessed place, for it gives me the space and time that I need and I never feel quite alone in it, for I live with my memories of Cashel Rock, the village, the ruins and Maeve. And there is more, for it is my belief, my mad fancy perhaps, that somewhere in my warehouse, hidden behind the vast crates and packing cases, there is a door which opens onto a land of mists and, coming through the mists, the sound of fiddles and high-pitched laughter. I might hear the fiddle music and the laughter, but I can never find the door and I doubt I ever will.'

'Oh for God's sake! Were you really hoping to stumble across laughing fiddlers hiding behind a pile of crates filled with machine tools, bananas, or whatever? That is so sodding fey! Give over!'

Tom put out his hands apologetically.

'Lady, there is no need to jump down my throat. We

may take it that I was speaking figuratively. Putting aside my *fantasy* of the mist behind the lost door, you should know that warehousing can be a thing of great beauty, for, though it is not commonly known, it is both a science and an art. A well-run warehouse shelters a wonderfully intricate display of three-dimensional geometry in motion. As in a tangram puzzle, everything has to fit precisely. The pallets are — hang on. You do know what a pallet is?'

'Yes, of course. We sometimes get stuff delivered on pallets at Sotheby's.'

'OK, well then, the pallets are of standard sizes and they have their designated pallet racks stacked in colour-coded and numbered bays, and the forklifts that move backwards and forwards between them are eerily quiet in part of the slow-motion kinematics that is the life of the warehouse. But it is not just a matter of matching size to size, pallet to pallet rack, for the additional dimension is time and some of what has been delivered and stacked will be going out much sooner and maybe in greater quantities than stuff that the warehouse has taken in earlier. So, in the interest of efficiency, that is speed, it will need to be stacked closer to the docking doors, and the logistics of docking requires that the shortest pathways have to be plotted both for those deliveries that are destined to be stored for a long time and for those more recently arrived but scheduled to be going out soon. One could fancy that one is looking on the rearrangements of the molecular structures that form the stuff of the universe as one watches these blocks rising, falling and turning until they find their destined settings. Behind all the rise and fall of pallet blocks which are raised up or lifted down from their pallet racks, there are lifts echoing that rise and fall as they carry yet more blocks to be stored on the mezzanine. The inventories that must register all these movements look like complex algebraic equations. Their necessary calculations are abstract and yet they represent what is tangible and which has to serve human needs. We who work in such a place are its willing slaves. At least, that is when the place is busy, but, on a quiet day as the winter's afternoon shadows spread across the floor, the place seems more like some pharaoh's tomb with its attendant sarcophagi stacked all around me. Indeed, I should say…'

Molly interrupted again, 'You manage all that? No, now I think about it, I am guessing that you are not really the manager are you? I can hear it in your voice that you are not so very grand.'

'To be honest, no, you are right. You have a good ear. I am more of a day-watchman, though I like to think of myself as doubling up as the warehouse's poet in residence.'

She had listened stony-faced to his account of the mystic warehouse and by now it was obvious that she was impatient to talk about herself. He shrugged, 'Your turn. Tell me about the men who were brought to ruin in your bed.'

'I'll not be defined by the men I slept with! The hell with that! It is not what I want to talk about.'

'So if you don't want to be defined by those men, why did you rush to tell the group about these ill-fated fellows? And what *do* you want to talk about?'

'Oh, I had to say something, but fucking is not that fucking important to me. So, to be brisk, the first man, no he was more of a boy really, is either in prison, just out of prison, or just about to go back into prison. The second man I married and then he vanished into thin air. The third went mad and had to be shut up in a lunatic asylum. The fourth I left, but he continues hopelessly and tiresomely to stalk me. I don't want to say anything about the fifth man — that might even be dangerous. OK? Now what I really want to talk about is history and adventure. Have you ever heard of the Countess Markiewicz?'

'You are talking to an Irishman.'

'Yes, sorry. The Countess wore silk kimonos. She drove a coach and four. She had a Colt revolver with which she practised by shooting the tops off candles. She took part in the Easter Rising and she was sentenced to death before being pardoned, but ten years later she died in a pauper's ward. That is a life! I want to have adventures! I want to become an adventuress, though it is hard to have adventures if one does not have much money. So right now I may be a kind of superior floorwalker in an auction house, but I am saving up to become an adventuress like Markiewicz, Lola Montez or Milady de Winter.'

'Who is this Lola?'

She explained that Lola Montez was a lady who became famous as a Spanish dancer. She had an affair with Alexandre Dumas. Her second husband was killed in a duel outside Paris. After that she moved to Munich where she met King Ludwig of Bavaria who asked her if her breasts were real. She tore open her bodice to prove that they were and after that became his mistress and then Ludwig made her a countess. This was not popular with the Bavarians and Ludwig was forced to abdicate, and Lola moved to London but then she and the Englishman she had married had to flee the country because a charge of bigamy was impending… and then… and then… scandal followed scandal.

Tom thought that Lola Montez, who brought bad luck to every man she associated with, might indeed be Molly's role model. Meanwhile Molly had moved on, 'One of my first essays at Oxford was on…'

'You were at Oxford?'

'Oh yes. I am not stupid, though my tutors certainly thought I was. I well remember my first proper essay…'

She remembered it all too well. She even remembered the exact title: 'How successful were the fiscal policies of Philip IV of France?' In her essay she had shown how the King, bizarrely known as 'Philip the Fair', no longer heeded the advice of the honourable old nobility and instead used clever civil servants like Marigny to get rid of feudalism. The King was 'neither a man, nor a beast, but a statue'. His fiscal policy was simple. It was to make as much money for himself as possible. To that end, the King and his pen-pushing ministers debased currency, so that everybody had less money. Then he confiscated people's silver to make new coins and revalued the currency, so that everybody had even less money. (How did that work?)

Tom listened with growing impatience and incredulity. How could this woman care so much about things that had happened centuries ago? It was not as if this French King had seized any of her property. But it seemed that for Molly history was a form of spectator sport and she was there in the stands, booing the baddies and trying to shout her support for the doomed goodies. She would not be stopped and she went on about how Philip seized the property of the Jews and taxed the clergy. Then he arrested the Knights Templars, seized their property and had them burnt at the stake on the trumped-up charge of heresy. From his funeral pyre the Grand Master of the Templars, Jacques de Molay, cursed the King and his ministers and summoned them to the tribune of Heaven and the last thing the horrified crowd could see of Jacques de Molay was his blackened hand pointing to heaven.'

Molly's voice grew louder as she reached the climax of her narrative and quite a few people had turned to look at her. Now she raised her right hand and pointed to the ceiling of Cranks. It was as if she was now cursing vegetarianism. People looked away embarrassed.

'Within a year of Jacques de Molay's curse the King and his evil minister Marigny were dead. What good had all their money done them? It could hardly be used to bribe the Judge in the hereafter.'

God and then Molly had judged the evil King. It seemed that everything that was important in Molly's life had happened hundreds of years ago before she was born and she went on and on about what she saw as the fiscal policies of fourteenth-century France. Well, according to her, they were called 'fiscal policies', but really it was just greed dressed up as sound economic measures. Today's historians could not see that it was their duty to denounce evil whenever they saw it. Dons worshipped the power of certain medieval Kings for their success in employing modern management techniques in order to hasten the end of the Middle Ages.

'My tutor asked me in a patronising voice if I was sure that I was in the right subject. Of course I was sure. It was god-bollocking her who wasn't. She gave me gamma minus for that essay and said that she was being kind. Well, Fuckadoodledoo!'

Then Molly went on a new riff about Boadicea, the pirate Anne Bonney and Lady Emma Hamilton. The other thing about Molly was that she always liked to back the losers, such as Boadicea, the cavaliers, or Anne Bonney who ended up in prison and would have been hung if she had not been pregnant. From time to time she surveyed the restaurant as she talked. Then, 'Look at the drab clothes everyone is wearing in here. All those blacks and browns! And things were better when men wore swords, for then there was the spice of challenge and danger in the streets. But, as well as danger, there used to be honour, courtesy and ceremony. Now it's efficiency, sound economy and all things boring.'

Molly had taken three-quarters of their hour setting out her view of history. All that natter must be some kind of displacement activity, though it was pleasant to see her so animated. Sadly, she had shown no real interest in warehousing. Tom told her that he did not think that what they had been talking about over lunch really counted as co-counselling. Though he had been paying full attention, he could not see that anything she had said gave as much as a hint as to why she had joined an encounter group. She nodded in agreement, 'Bugger that! We will try and do better next time. Perhaps then I will tell you about my men.'

As they came out of Cranks, she looked left and right. Then, 'Can you walk me back to Sotheby's?'

'I'm sorry. I'm running late and I really ought to catch a bus now. My boss did not give me much time off.'

The next minute she had hailed a taxi and darted into it. Looking round, Tom saw behind him a young man who was looking furious. Doubtless he had hailed the cab first. Tom made his way over to Piccadilly, caught the 88 bus to Vauxhall and walked on from there to the warehouse. He and Molly had wasted their lunch in avoiding the truth. But then, why not? Lies are usually nicer, kinder things than truths.

CHAPTER THREE

Molly arrived at the second encounter session flustered and out of breath. Under her canary yellow raincoat she was wearing a green shift dress and a cloche hat. Almost everybody else was wearing glum winter clothing. The exception was Ferdie, the man with wiry black hair who had been Tom's neighbour in the previous session. He was in full evening dress. The session started late and, as the group waited for Leon, they discussed whether they should all take their clothes off again, before deciding against it, since they had already done that, been there and, as it were, lost the T-shirt. When Leon did arrive, he entered carrying a long and broad white strip of cloth.

'What is that Leon?'

'It is my winding sheet. I want to know what it will be like when I am dead.'

Philip was about to say something, but Ferdie cut in, 'Hey, great! Just lie down there and we will give you the funeral you deserve.'

Sally started to wrap the cloth round the recumbent Leon, starting with his feet. For a few minutes Ferdie stood silent behind Leon's head. He was thinking. Then he started, 'Brothers and Sisters of Quaesitor, we are gathered here this evening to bid our beloved colleague, Leon, farewell. I'd like to share with you these thoughts.

'Though we felt we hardly knew him before he went and died on us, he will be greatly missed. We shall not see his like again, not in this basement anyway. He was always ready to help our group to which he contributed so much. As you know, he had been seriously ill for some time. He fought bravely, but the cancer turned out to be a tougher and more ruthless fighter than he was and at last it came upon him like a thief in the night and, piff-paff, that was the end of him! "Cut is the branch that might have grown full straight and burned is Apollo's laurel bough." And now I think that it is for me to invite you to come up one by one and pay your own personal tributes to our dear departed Leon.'

Meanwhile, the wrapping had been going slowly, since it was an awkward business, as Sally and Fiona, her of the 'manky body', kept having to get Leon to roll over in order to slide the winding sheet under him. Also Melanie was lying at Leon's feet sobbing unconvincingly. Nick was raising and lowering his hands in lamentation. Josephine was sitting in a corner with her hands over her ears and humming to herself. (Later they learnt that she believed that talking about cancer, or even thinking about it, could bring it on.) The rest of the group were looking at one another, all reluctant to be the first to offer a funeral tribute.

'Perhaps our beloved leader, Philip, would like to lead us in this memorial tribute,' Ferdie suggested. But it was Jerome who staggered to his feet.

'Actually I think he is well out of it since...'

But he was cut off by Philip who bellowed, 'Stop this

nonsense, all of you, now, immediately! Quaesitor is not cheap and it is your money you are wasting! Let Leon out of that stupid sheet and get back into the circle.'

Ferdie insisted on adding, '"And say to all the world, this was a man." But hist! He breathes yet!'

'Yes, he is blinking his eyes,' Melanie confirmed.

Then Ferdie sat down quickly and Melanie followed. Leon, who was looking furious since he had hoped for something more serious, threw off his grave-cloth and rejoined the circle, remarking as he did so, 'The rest of you have thirty, forty, maybe fifty years ahead of you. I have at most two.'

Once they were all back in what were supposed to be their proper places and Philip had calmed down, he continued, 'From now on no trophies are to be brought to the group sessions. So no teddy bears, no urns full of ashes, no stuffed animals, no er...'

Raymond jumped in to finish the list for him, 'No firearms, flick knives, uncooked meats, pornography, uncut diamonds or large quantities of foreign currency.'

Philip sighed and then got them doing ten minutes of communal humming in order to help everyone calm down and get on the same wavelength. Then he went round the room checking on how the co-counselling sessions had gone. He got a lot of vague but affirmative responses. One had to learn to affirm the identity and needs of others. All so much blah, until he got to Tom who said, 'I am sure that I am speaking for Molly as well as myself when I say that we cannot stand each other and, so far at least, we don't really seem to have any problems that can be resolved by talking them through.'

Molly nodded emphatically.

'Well, I suppose that I could take over the co-counselling of Molly,' said Philip tentatively.

The protests of Tom and Molly were simultaneous.

'That would leave me without a co-counselling partner!'

'I very much enjoy being co-counselled by a man who does not like me! It makes a welcome change from men who like me so much that they just want to screw me.'

Philip shrugged and said, 'My guess is that what you two are experiencing is what analysts call negative transference. Superficially what occurs is that the person being counselled attributes negative characteristics to the person who is the therapist or counsellor, but what is really happening is that a bad internal feeling with respect to a parent, a marital partner or other bad object from the past is externalised and attributed to the counsellor. The intense feelings experienced in that past are thereby displaced. Despite its problems, this is the beginning of a healing process, so, though it is called negative transference, it is quite a positive thing. Just remember that it's not part of the problem it's part of the solution.'

'Gosh!' said Jerome. 'I think I keep getting negative transferences all the time.'

Philip then went out and came back with a top hat. Raymond sighed, 'We forgot to include hats in the list of banned trophies.'

'That's my hat!' said Ferdie.

But Philip now distributed pencils and paper and got everybody to write down their greatest fear and put it in the hat. Then he'd read the answers out and they'd have to guess which of them had written which fear. The answers were as follows: spiders, death, not understanding what other people are saying, the murderous man I am having an affair with, heights, dementia, flying, sex, death (again), artistic failure, redundancy and big dogs. Though many guesses were made, Philip let the confessions remain anonymous, even though it was easy to guess the authors of at least a few of the confessions.

Ferdie reclaimed his hat and gazed uncertainly into it. Then he gave a cry of triumph, 'Aha! I knew I'd put it somewhere!' And he produced a stuffed rabbit out of the hat. There was scattered applause.

But, as Raymond was quick to point out, 'Stuffed animals are on the list of banned trophies.'

Philip was determined once more to bring the group back to order. He told them that now they had externalised their fears by writing them down, they were to exorcise those fears by screaming for as long as they could. Thus their demons would be driven out of the basement. And so things continued.

Tom (artistic failure, of course) was taking careful mental notes on how the group interactions were proceeding. He thought that there was perhaps a kind of inevitability about group dynamics. Though Philip could be seen as the leader, he was trying not to be and, in the absence of a formally declared leader, Raymond and Ferdie, like rutting stags, were contesting for hegemony within the group. Josephine, the one who did not want to hear about cancer, was setting herself up to be the group's outsider and eventually scapegoat, while Jerome was settling into his role as their comedian. Also Tom guessed that Raymond and Melanie were already sleeping together. He looked much happier for it. Molly (probably afraid of the man she was having an affair with) seemed to be more of an observer than a participant in the group. As for Philip, despite his best efforts, he was becoming more and more authoritarian and, with his narrow face and shoulder-length hair, he looked somewhat like a medieval inquisitor. In the end the great thing about the group was that everybody had a turn at being made to feel that they were interesting and in this way everybody's narcissism was indulged. Meanwhile the troubles of the world, including Edward Heath's impending assault on the Health Service, the Biafran War, the Israelis in Lebanon and the starving in sub-Saharan Africa, could be comfortably ignored.

Suddenly, Nick, seeing how deep in thought Tom was, pointed at him and said, 'He says so little. I think he's the spy in our group.'

Tom smiled, 'The name's Byrne. Tom Byrne. But of course it would be ridiculous to be a spy in an encounter group. Spies are supposed to discover secrets and there are no secrets amongst us. At least there are not supposed to be.'

But Ferdie said, 'A man is not what he thinks he is. He is what he hides.'

(That was baffling.)

Philip followed this up with, 'Tell us a secret, Tom.'

'OK. I do not want to become a better person and I have not joined this group in order to become one.'

The group, baffled by Ferdie's mysterious dictum and by Tom's equally mysterious confession, let the topic drop. Instead of a meditation, this session ended with Philip briskly instructing them in tai chi, so that they might experience the flux of yin and yang flowing through them. Tom and Molly arranged to meet again the Thursday after next. But she said that she thought that Cranks was no longer safe for her. So it should be *Le Macabre*, a coffee bar, in Meard Street. Then she waved him away and she paused to talk to Ferdie.

CHAPTER FOUR

Tom was so bemused by the coffins that served as tables, the skulls that served as candle-holders and the prancing skeletons on the walls that he did not notice Molly behind him until she tapped him on the shoulder. This time she was wearing jeans and a black leather jacket over a silk blouse. While her coffee was being made, she went over to *Le Macabre*'s juke box and chose something from *Kindertotenlieder*.

Finally she sat down with her coffee and Tom looked enquiringly at her.

'I know this place is kind of weird, but it's a *lieu de memoire*. Ten years ago or so I came here with my vanished husband. Sorry I didn't accompany you to the tube after the last session. I stopped to talk to Ferdie. He's quite interesting.' (Unlike you was unspoken.) 'He is a professional conjuror. When I was a little girl, I used to love conjuring. It was so brightly coloured like fireworks and heraldry. Are you sure that you are not an agent of SMERSH or the CIA?'

Tom smiled, 'I wish I was. That way I might be earning a lot more money than I am now.'

'Pity. That would make things more interesting. The sessions could do with some livening up. I am not sure that

I can put up with yet more of its feel-good stuff. You always look as though you've got something to hide and that you're investigating something.'

Tom shrugged and said, 'I'm sure that everyone in the group has got plenty to hide, including us. Anyway this time we must try and do the co-counselling properly and this time it is you first.'

She sighed exaggeratedly, 'So be it. At the risk of sounding arrogant — but the hell with that, since I have plenty to be arrogant about — my curse is that I am too beautiful and men are under the delusion that beauty promises happiness. I don't think that it has been the case for them and it certainly hasn't for me. My story…'

Tom interrupted:

'May she be granted beauty and yet not
Beauty to make a stranger's eye distraught,
Or hers before a looking-glass, for such,
Being made beautiful overmuch,
Consider beauty a sufficient end,
Lose natural kindness and maybe
The heart-revealing intimacy
That chooses right, and never find a friend.'

'Is that one of your poems? If so, it is quite good.'

'Alas, Yeats got there first.'

'Oh well. My story is a strange one and perhaps this is the right kind of place for it. I acquired my first boyfriend while I was still at school in Guildford. Ned was rather good-looking and he was besotted with me. He kept wanting to give me things, but he didn't have much money, so he took to shoplifting the things he thought I might fancy. The second time he was caught, he went to prison. I used to visit him there. When he came out, we resumed our relationship and he resumed the thieving. The second time he went to prison I gave him up. He still writes to me, especially when he is in prison as he has no one else to write to, but I think the truth is that he is now more in love with thieving than he ever was with me.

'Then I went up to Oxford to read history and in my second year I met two undergraduates who were in their third year doing English Literature. They were both terrifyingly brilliant. Lancelyn was the handsome one, but, as I eventually found out, he was scared stiff of women and so somehow I ended up with his good friend Bernard and, after Bernard got a brilliant first in his finals and was given a research fellowship at All Souls, I married him. He certainly was not afraid of women. So I became an academic's wife which was a bit boring and we hadn't much money and he became horribly depressed after his first book — his only book — got a nasty review. Still I was doing my best. But then he vanished…'

'What do you mean he vanished?'

'Just that. He took a suitcase of clothes, plus copies of his book, which, by the way, was an academic study of ghost stories. He also took all the housekeeping money. He left no note and apparently had told no one of his intentions.'

'Where do you think he is now?'

'Who knows? He might be dead, maybe murdered, or dead by his own hand. Maybe he got lost and starved to death in a remote mountain region. Or he joined the Foreign Legion. He could be playing the piano in a brothel in Macao.

Or he could have changed his name, married again and found fulfilment working as a greengrocer. I don't know and by now I don't care. That was almost ten years ago. After seven years I applied to the courts to have him declared dead. That was a time-consuming and expensive business.'

'But you can't just lose a husband in a fit of absent-mindedness! You must have left him somewhere. Did you try the Lost Person's Office?'

She smiled humourlessly and continued, 'His friend, Lancelyn, who had got a post teaching English Literature in the University of St Andrews, turned up on a visit to Oxford soon after Bernard had vanished and I asked if I could accompany him back to Scotland. I was adrift with no money for the rent or anything else and besides I liked him, but, though I liked him a lot, perhaps even loved him, he certainly was weird. As I say, he was scared stiff of women. Like Bernard he had a creepy obsession with ghosts, though he did not seem to be as afraid of them as he was of women. He was quite rich and he had a huge collection of books. But they were not normal books. They were books about sorcery, earth-eating, non-existent politicians, knife-throwing, genital mutilation, head-shrinking techniques, edible architecture, out-of-body experiences, the origins of human speech in the croaking of frogs, stuff like that. Quite a few of the books were pornographic and he also kept a collection of naughty photo magazines beside his bed. Sex for him was something that primarily existed in books and magazines. What happened next may sound a bit strange and it certainly turned out to be a mistake. I had the mad idea that I might cure him by some kind of psychodrama. I wanted to ween him off pornography and masturbation. You have to remember that this was years before Quaesitor had been thought of, or sophisticated counselling techniques had been developed. I enlisted the help of a friend of his in the English Department, who was called Jaimie, to join us in sexual psychodramas. I suppose in a way we were pioneers, except we really did not know what we were doing and what we did made him worse, though we never guessed how much worse until it was very nearly too late. One day he bought a big can of paraffin, intending to set the house on fire while we were all inside. Happily he was intercepted in time. I tried to visit him in the mental hospital in Dundee but they would not let me.

'So first I had lost my husband and then Lancelyn, whom I had adored despite all his kinkiness, had ended up horribly damaged. Moreover, by now Jaimie had become sexually obsessed with me. I really wish some bloody scientist would invent a man-repellent perfume. So it was a bad time in St Andrews, a really terrible time. Yet, all the same, it was also a good time, in a way the best of all times, since at least things were happening and it was passion that was making them happen. Things have been quieter in London, even though I fear that the consequences of what happened in Oxford and St Andrews have not yet fully worked themselves out. And now the sixties are over. How did that happen? How could it have happened? I thought that the good music would go on and on forever. But The Beatles seem played out, Diana Ross has given her last concert and Janis Joplin is dead. The sixties have gone like an iridescent bubble and with it all the colour has been leached out of Britain. I was young then and I suppose a bit mad.

'Anyway, Jaimie. He is still a lecturer in the English

Department in St Andrews. He has published a study of a mad writer called James Hogg and more recently a book entitled *The Problem of Evil in the Scottish Novel*. It was a book he was uniquely qualified to write, being Scottish, evil and a hell of a problem. Even so, though evil, he was sort of fun. After the rumpus about Lancelyn's nervous breakdown, I left St Andrews and moved down to London and I said goodbye to Jaimie, or so I thought. But now, whenever his academic commitments will let him, he comes down to London and he stalks me. The doorman at Sotheby's is under instructions not to let him in. It has been going on for years and makes me extremely jumpy.

'When I first arrived in London the only place I could find to live in was a squat. Then I sought the help of someone I knew at Oxford, a friend of Bernard and Lancelyn… I suppose there is no real harm in your knowing his Christian name at least. He is Marcus, a senior executive, a high flyer. It was Marcus who introduced me to Sotheby's and got me somewhere decent to live and he moved me again when Jaimie found out where I was living. Marcus was happily married to Janet, a slightly older woman with two children from an earlier marriage. The trouble was that the more Marcus helped me and the more he saw of me, the more he liked what he saw. We had an affair. We were very discreet and Janet would never have guessed. But Jaimie, my shadow, discovered what was going on and he wrote to Janet denouncing us. There was a divorce and Marcus was barred from ever seeing the step-children of whom he had become very fond and they had loved him in return. Janet, of course, hates me. Marcus and I live separately, but he visits frequently. He used to be a gentle, rather wistful character, but now that he has taken to drink he can be pretty violent. I think that "mistress" is a beautiful word, but the reality is not so beautiful. So there you are.' She smiled. 'Be careful, Tom. You now.'

'But I still want to know who cursed you. Was it God, or your first boyfriend, or who?'

'Oh, I was just speaking figuratively — like you with your merry, high-pitched fiddlers. I just wanted to warn off all the men in the group. So now, it's you and I want to know about you and not more about the warehouse as a work of art.'

It was his turn to sigh, 'There is so little of me. So it will have to be Yeats. I live under his shadow. He has possessed me, or rather his poetry has. It is because of him that I must be a poet and it is because of him that I cannot be a poet. His verses are so good that it seems to me that some of them at least must have a supernatural source. There is a portal, a door with mist and laughter behind it if you will, which he found, but I cannot, since he is blocking my way — or perhaps it is Maeve. Perhaps it is she who guards the door. I had thought that if I could get away from her, then I might find the door. But nothing has worked out. I don't suppose that you are familiar with the old Celtic practice of *taghairm*?'

Molly shook her head.

'*Taghairm* literally means "spiritual echo". It is a Celtic form of divination, of seeking inspiration in which one wraps oneself in a bullock's hide before lying down behind a waterfall and then, mixed in with the roaring of the water, the sought-for inspiration will come. I am so desperate that I am actually thinking of going to a butcher and arranging the purchase of a bullock's hide before seeking out the right sort of waterfall.

But then again, I am thinking that the portal may be in Cashel after all, and I should seek Maeve's pardon and beg her to give me the gift of creating magic with words.'

'Oh, for Christ's sake! Why don't you just sit down and write some poetry as best you can? That sort of thing comes with practice and, if you practise, you may in time produce brilliantly powerful poetry. No need to waste money on the purchase of the hide of an old bullock.'

'But I have been practising and, though most of what I have written has gone straight into the wastepaper basket, the best of my poems have been published in two slim volumes.'

'But last time you told me that you were not a poet! You presented yourself as just a warehouseman.'

'Perhaps you did not grasp my meaning. I do not regard myself as a poet, since I don't think it is enough for someone to write some poems in order to qualify as a poet. Children, idiots and the composers of advertising jingles can make verses. My poetry is just not good enough to validate any status as a poet. I paid for the publication of the first volume myself. The second volume Carcanet took, but neither has had any reviews and my poems have not brought in enough money for me to buy a cup of coffee. If I had the money, I'd buy every unsold copy and burn them.'

'I would like to see your poems.'

'Perhaps you shall. I have plenty of complimentary copies which I have not yet got round to burning.'

Molly sat back, perhaps a little stunned, at the revelation that she was having coffee and croissants with a published poet.

So Tom was free to ramble on about Maeve, who resembled

a banshee, for banshees were traditionally held to have red hair. Her beauty was a clear manifestation of the supernatural. Molly said that she would very much like to meet Maeve. Then more generally Tom talked about the decorum of dealing with the spirit world and how the spirits, or inspirations if one preferred, were most commonly encountered in twilight. And why should fairies not exist? After all they had a function in human society, since they offered a refuge from the miseries of everyday life and they maintained a form of spiritual healing that was much wiser and more ancient than group therapy. Not, mind you, that they looked like the mimsy little winged figures one saw in Victorian paintings. Fairies looked like normal-sized human beings...

Eventually, Molly said, 'I am thinking that by the time Tom the Poet returns to Cashel and he has that meeting with his Maeve on the slopes of the Mount, her knees will be too arthritic for her to kneel before you, and the same will be true for you too, for you will be too old and tired to do any kneeling, and anyway it will turn out that she has married the local butcher. Now, if you are not good enough to be a proper poet, whatever that may be, what are you going to do about it? And, given what you have been saying about ancient fairy therapy, what may I ask are you doing in the encounter group?'

Tom was silent a long time. Then, 'OK, I will be straight with you. I have not given up on the poetry, but I thought I would try a new form. I thought that I would try to write a verse drama, like Yeats, T. S. Eliot and Christopher Fry, and, when I read about Quaesitor, I thought that the group set-up would provide perfect material for a verse drama.'

Before he had finished speaking Molly had burst into

peals of laughter. In such a morbid and shadowy setting, the effect was eerie. When she could speak, 'Sorry. Sorry. It's not what you think it is. I am not laughing at you. I am laughing at us, I suppose. That's pretty much the same as why I am in the group. I am a novelist and I have been looking for a good setting for my next novel.'

'You are a novelist! Should I have heard of you?'

'Well, no. Not yet. My first novel, *The Rod and the Knout* will be published in a few weeks' time. You must come to the launch. Just don't come near me while Marcus is there. Now we really should not be spending time together. Our projects are too alike.'

'Yes, and there is probably someone else in the group who is hoping to get a grand opera out of it.'

'And yet another person who is working on a *haiku* about group therapy.'

Molly was right. They dared not talk about their perceptions of the group or about their creative projects. Tom's ideas about his verse drama were terribly vague. He had thought of a psychodrama that would be something like Sartre's *Huis Clos*, only with more people in it. Then he had toyed with the idea of presenting the encounter group as a kind of contemporary re-enactment of the Last Supper. Philip would be Jesus who tries to lead his followers into self-realisation, but he tells them that, 'There is one among us who will betray me.' *Murder in the Cathedral* might be another model. Then again a murder mystery set in Quaesitor's basement seemed a possibility. None of this could be discussed with Molly. Besides he was now beginning to sense that Molly herself might make a better subject for a verse drama than any encounter group. She was a modern Medea. As she moved from man to man she was someone who was ruthless enough to kill her own children, if she ever were to have any. They talked for another quarter of an hour before leaving *Le Macabre*.

CHAPTER FIVE

Philip was increasingly confident at the third session and Tom was toying with the idea of casting him as some kind of Svengali figure who used mesmerism and various tricks to gain control over a group of innocents. It was also obvious that he fancied Molly (who this time was wearing a kaftan). Now Philip was going round getting everyone in turn to 'affirm' as many people in the group as they could, but when he got to Molly, she pointed to Tom and said, 'I'm sorry, but I have to tell you all that I cannot possibly affirm that man over there. He told me that he was a poet, but there is no bone of poetry in him. So I have had my suspicions and after our last co-counselling session I followed him and saw him enter a police station and a little later he came out with another policeman who was obviously one of his mates. Tom is a snoop. Though why a police spy? Why the police should want to spy on us I cannot guess.'

Tom put his hands together as in a gesture of prayer, 'It's a fair cop and she's got me bang to rights. It's quite stressful working undercover and it's a relief to be straight with you at last. And I have to apologise to you all. You are good people and through these sessions I think I have learned how to be a better policeman. In mitigation for the snooping, my plea is that I was not assigned to infiltrate and spy on this group as such. My job was to keep tabs on Molly. She is known to be a witch and is suspected of having connections with a coven of Satanists on the Isle of Man. We naturally wondered what she might be doing in a therapeutic group. Perhaps she will be good enough to tell us.'

Molly looked abashed, 'Well, yes, it is true that I am a witch, but listen, hey, wise up! Witches are good people and over the centuries they have worked hard to improve the conditions of the poor and enhance the status of women. Historically, witches have always been the voices of the oppressed. They were able to provide women with comfort and herbal remedies which were denied to them by the quack doctors of the Middle Ages. What is really amazing is how similar the work we do in the covens is to what you are doing at Quaesitor. What I would propose…'

Philip cut her off, 'It is not funny. I think that the two of you had better leave.'

There were murmurs of approval. Molly spat on the back of her left fist before extending the little finger and the index finger in the cursing gesture of the *mano cornuto*. Tom shrugged apologetically and followed her out of the room.

Upstairs in the lobby Tom presented Molly with his two slim volumes and Molly gave him a proof copy of *The Rod and the Knout*.

'That was fun,' she said. They were laughing as they made their way to the tube station, but then Molly stopped, 'Christ! It's him!' (No, not Him.)

There was a line of taxis queued opposite the tube station.

'Come with me, please,' she begged as she took Tom's hand and they ran to the taxi at the front of the queue. She shouted as they boarded it, 'Bishop's Road, Highgate, please.'

The driver grunted and the cab moved slowly off and turned left into Finchley Road. Molly sank back in her seat. Then she looked out of the rear window and asked the cabbie to turn off left. He did so. Then she asked him to turn right. He grunted and did so. By now they were heading up Loudoun Road. Molly looked back again before leaning forward to talk to the cabbie, 'Do you see that taxi behind? It is following us. Forget about Highgate. There's fifty pounds for you on top of whatever the fare will be if you can shake him off.'

'Now you're talking, lady! Fasten your seat belts!'

'Is that Marcus behind us?' Tom wanted to know.

The cabbie, who was wreathed in smiles, turned to them and said, 'We'll take it slowly at first to throw them off guard.'

Molly agreed, before turning to Tom again, 'No, Marcus knows where I live and he can turn up and beat me up any time he feels like it. No, it's Jaimie. I can't think how he tracked me down to the encounter group. Maybe he followed me from my publisher a few weeks back. My publisher is also his publisher. I have been careless, because it was term time and I thought that he would be in Scotland. He must not find out where I live. Really…'

But at this point she broke off and she and Tom lurched forward as the cab did a very sharp U-turn and now accelerated down Loudoun Road.

'The Austin FX4 is not built for speed. Seventy miles per hour max, but they all have an admirably small turning circle.'

He had turned to give them another big smile and he would

keep looking back at them as he continued to accelerate.

'Are we still aiming for Highbury?' he shouted.

Tom shouted back, 'No. Battersea Dogs Home and drive like hell!'

There was a distant screeching sound behind them and furious hooting. With some difficulty the taxi behind them had also managed the U-turn and was still in pursuit. The cabbie stuck his head out of his window to look back.

'I don't know this one, but he's good,' he said.

Molly gripped Tom's hand. Her eyes glittered and she was breathing fast through her mouth. She was in a transport of delight. Now she wanted to talk about an exciting book she had just been reading about Mary Queen of Scots by Lady Somebody or Other. She, Mary — not Lady Somebody or Other — had married the Dauphin of France, but, soon after he became King, he died from an ear abscess, and then, after she returned as a widow to Scotland, she married Lord Darnley. Then Mary had an affair with her secretary, David Rizzio. But Darnley and a gang of Protestant lords came upon Mary and Rizzio having dinner together and they cut Rizzio down. A few years later Darnley's house was blown up and he was found dead n the garden. Then...

Then the driver looked back again to inform them, 'I'm not a great reader myself. I prefer films. Did either of you see *Bullitt*?'

They had not. So the driver continued, 'It came out a couple of years ago. I've seen it three times. It's got Steve McQueen in it and a terrific car chase. He's driving a — woops! I forgot they made this bit one-way, but there is nothing to do but go forward. Say your prayers lady — and you too sir!'

There was more furious hooting as he concentrated on negotiating his way down the one-way street and Molly was briefly able to pick up on Mary Queen of Scots and how, after Darnley's murder, she married his murderer, the Earl of Bothwell, but there was a rebellion of the Scottish nobility and Bothwell was imprisoned and went mad in prison before he died...

But once out of the one-way street the cabbie was able to rejoin the conversation, 'Now I've forgotten what kind of car it was in *Bullitt*. Doesn't matter. Maybe a Ford Mustang. Anyway, not the sort of make that's right for a London taxi. McQueen though, he's a looker and tough. He used to be in the Marines. Mind you, as an actor he is perhaps a bit monotonous. Do you think he did his own driving or was it stuntmen? Oh, I forgot, you haven't seen the film. You should. The car chase in *Bullitt* is terrific. The way the cars bounced up and down was terrific. The trouble is that London doesn't have hills the way San Francisco does. Though, come to think of it, Highgate is good for hills. Are you sure, you won't change your mind and we can head back to Highgate? Mind you, if we did, it would probably wreck my suspension, so perhaps let's not. Oh, I forgot to ask. Have the people in the cab behind got firearms?'

'I don't think so,' said Molly.

'Have either of you?'

'No.'

'Ah! Just as well, I suppose. Uh-oh, a red light coming. Time for another prayer, lady!'

Molly resumed her slightly garbled account of the bloody career of Mary Queen of Scots. Tom shut his eyes. He was going to die holding the hand of a beautiful but silly woman.

When he opened his eyes again he had no idea where they were, except that they must be heading down towards the Thames. As they got closer to the river, the faint wisps of mist that had been noticeable in St John's Wood had thickened into a dense fog. Finally, 'Lost him!' cried the taxi driver. 'Maybe his cab crashed in flames like in *Bullitt*.'

'More likely his passenger ran out of money,' Tom muttered.

The drive now continued in silence. They crossed the river at Vauxhall and soon arrived at the Dogs Home. Tom and Molly got out and argued at its entrance, 'You can't possibly live here!'

'No, but it's only a short walk to my flat and I need the air.'

'I was hoping you would invite me up for coffee or something. I would like to see your place.'

'I think I have had enough excitement for one evening,' he replied gravely.

Meanwhile the cabbie had got out and presented Molly with his card.

'If you or any of your friends want a car chase, I'm your man. Any time lady.'

Just as he was getting in and about to drive off, Tom stopped him, 'Please take this lady home, back to her address in Highgate.'

Molly scowled at Tom, it was a really lovely scowl, and said, 'Heigh ho, I must be losing my magical power to seduce.'

As she was reluctantly re-entering the cab, he asked, 'What would have happened if your evil Scotsman had caught up with us?'

'I don't know. Probably nothing. But it was fun, wasn't it?'

He walked away without replying. He resented the fact that he had been hustled into someone else's adventure. He certainly did not want her or any of her deranged men friends to know exactly where he lived. Then he wondered if it was possible that she had set up the taxi chase? Yes, it was conceivable. Anything was conceivable. He felt as though he had been led into a hall of mirrors. He had no desire to become an adventurer, only a poet.

Looking down from the window of his flat, he could see almost nothing of the park across the road, except the bare branches that ran like black veins through the fog. Should he write to Maeve about the recent strange events? She never wrote back. The hell with Maeve! He poured himself a whisky. If he drank enough, he might fall asleep and just possibly dream of her, though that happened less frequently now. Moreover, there had been a time when he thought of Maeve every day and very nearly every waking hour. Now he found himself weeping. He wept for Maeve, or rather he wept because he could hardly remember what she looked like, apart from the hair, and he wept because he now knew that he no longer cared for her. She probably had married a butcher or a grocer. The passing of the years in Cashel had pushed Tom aside. But then again it was possible she was dead... as for himself, his heart was dead and in time the rest of him would follow. The horns of Elfland calling him back to Ireland were getting fainter yet. 'Blow bugles, answer echoes, dying, dying, dying.' This was his fifth winter in London. Still in his twenties and he was already saying goodbye to a 'land of lost

47

content', also known as the 'country of the young':

> *'Where nobody gets old and godly and grave,*
> *Where nobody gets old and crafty and wise,*
> *Where nobody gets old and bitter of tongue;*
> *And she is still there, busied with a dance.'*

There should be no need for him to return to Ireland. He was sure that fairies were present everywhere, even in London, which was above all, of course, a place brought to ruin by vulgarity and greed. But even here the fairies had created secret tracks through the city and he had been able to take long weekend and evening walks through a half-enchanted townscape. He believed that he could detect the fairies in sudden gusts of wind which caught up the autumn leaves in small tornados. There were also more tangible manifestations. Not all the players of the three-card Monte and their accomplices on Waterloo and Westminster Bridges looked entirely human. Then there were the suspect-looking sellers of hot chestnuts in front of the British Museum and beside the Tower of London, as well as the banshee mourners he thought he saw following funeral processions through the City. He was not mad. Though these things were visible only to the poet's eye, such hallucinations were not enough to make one a poet. Finally he settled in bed with *The Oxford Companion to Being Alone*. It was not what he had hoped for. It was full of famous writers going on about how lonely they were.

When he awoke next morning he knew that it was true that Maeve had left him and there was not even the wraith of her to keep him company. Now that he found himself so suddenly alone, he was bored. After last night's single shot of adrenaline, he was perhaps already hooked. The fog was still heavy on the park when he walked out to work at the warehouse. This time for the first time in years he walked alone, since the shadow of Maeve no longer accompanied him. His fellow warehousemen talked of little except sport and politics and, because he would not, they regarded him as slightly touched. In any case, one should never speak of the fairies to anyone. As the day-watchman at a weekend, there was little for him to do, but he registered the reassignment of unused pallets, and meanwhile he thought instead about his future verse drama, *The New Medea* (working title). But should it be set in modern times? He needed to know more about Medea's modern model — that is he needed to know more about Molly.

CHAPTER SIX

A few evenings later Tom picked up the proof copy of *The Rod and the Knout* off the floor and started to read. Somewhat like that taxi driver, Tom wasn't much of a one for reading novels. Unlike poetry, fiction was not true. Reading such artificially constructed lies was, he thought, an acquired skill. *The Rod and the Knout* was set in Holy Russia sometime in the nineteenth or twentieth-century. Natasha was ravishing, impetuous, arrogant, passionate and loved to dance. She was married to the gentle, scholarly Alexei Checherin who busied himself with trying to improve the lot of the *muzhik*s. (What the hell was a *muzhik*?) In addition to all her other qualities, Natasha was also bored and looking for adventure. Then it was her ill fate to encounter Merdyakov, the cherubic-faced, favourite disciple of Rasputin and a dedicated sadist, as well as skilled mesmerist. He tricked Natasha into sleeping with Alexei's brother, Konstantin, a brooding existentialist philosopher. Having done so, Merdyakov then blackmailed her into sleeping with him and he proceeded to initiate her into Old Russian sex games. It was all very confusing, particularly as the large cast of characters seemed to have several names. Tom had gone on for twenty pages thinking that Alexei and Sasha were two different people. It was clear that there was going to be a suicide, though whether it would be that of Konstantin, Alexei or Natasha was impossible to guess. After a while, Tom gave up reading and just turned the pages. There was lots of dancing, featuring waltzes, balletic leaps and Cossacks doing the *Hopak*. Everything seemed to happen in swirl of champagne and vodka. Come to that, the whole novel read as though it had been written by someone on lots of vodka.

Early on in Tom's reading, an invitation to the launch of *The Rod and the Knout* had fallen out of the book and it lay on the floor for several days. Eventually he was so bored that he picked it up and considered going to the launch. It would be an adventure, admittedly a very small one indeed, but he had never been to a book launch before. He would have to find something polite to say about the novel, but he could probably manage that. Meanwhile he was excruciatingly bored. What was he doing? Why did he do anything? He was superfluous to life and what he desired was to feel desire for something or somebody.

At last the evening of the launch came round. This was in the office of the long-established publishing firm of Barrington and Lane in Mecklenburgh Square. Molly was standing behind a table piled high with her novel. She looked pale and nervous. Seeing him enter, she gave him a surreptitious wave and shook her head. He should not come near. Tom guessed that the pink-faced, sweaty man in the double-breasted suit must be the big business executive, Marcus. While the throng were being served white wine, Molly and the hypothetical Marcus were starting to share a bottle of vodka. Of course Tom knew no one in the room apart from Molly and he ended up chatting aimlessly to a doctor who was similarly placed. The doctor had been commissioned by Barrington and Lane to write the first book in a series of novels that would be designed to be read by people with incipient dementia. The doctor's novel would come with a bookmark which had all the characters listed as in the cast of a play. But there was more to it than that. It was quite a skill to pitch the writing right. Not *he said* and *she said*, but *Not if you value your life*, threatened Ralph, his eyes glittering evilly, and *I don't know what you mean*, replied Hermione, the hostess of the party, as she nervously touched her blonde hair. Never *she opened the casket*, but *Hermione opened the casket in which her diamond necklace was usually to be found*.

Barrington bustled by. He was confident about this new venture, 'It's a niche market. Money in the bank!'

Tom said little. He was watching Molly. She was wearing an exotic-looking yellow and black trouser suit. It was the sort of thing that could have been worn on the set of Rimsky-Korsakov's *Scheherazade*. She was beautiful, but so what? Yeats, who spent his entire life worshipping female beauty, towards the end, described it as:

'*A strange unserviceable thing,*
A fragile, exquisite pale shell,
That the vast troubled waters bring
To the loud sands before the day has broken.'

Tom then found himself pressed close to an opinionated young man who was trying to impress a young woman by arguing that

Yeats had enslaved himself to the White Goddess and that was his tragedy. A couple on Tom's other side were enthusing about *The French Lieutenant's Woman* by John Fowles. Further away there was a gang of young men in suits and all of them with long hair. He guessed that they were the Sotheby's contingent as they clustered round the desk laughing and chatting with Molly. He heard the woman whom the opinionated man had been trying to impress say that it was really time for the book to be introduced and for there to be a reading. But they were still hoping for the arrival of Mortimer. Apparently Mortimer was the fiction editor at *The Times Literary Supplement* and he had promised the publisher that he would come to the launch. Without Mortimer the launch would have to be judged a failure.

Then the opinionated man said that he was pleased to see that Molly was young and her friends seemed fairly young too. The trouble with so many writers was that they hung on for too long. E. M. Forster, who was in his nineties when he died, had been a waste of space for decades. The books of old writers were crowding out the creations of the young and denying them the chance of publication. Doris Lessing, Olivia Manning, Vladimir Nabokov, Anthony Powell and the rest of them should back out gracefully. Going past the fiction shelves in a public library was like walking round a cemetery. *Death Comes For the Archbishop*, *The Death of a Hero*, *The Death of the Heart*. And old people did not just talk about their ailments. They wrote about them too. Proust was insufferable in that way and Joyce not that much better. Old writers got over-preoccupied first with illness and then death and the stories they wrote were dominated by that final full stop. Young and middle-aged readers should not have to put up with such stuff. Apparently the young man would have been published by now if it was not for the deadweight of tired novels published by old writers. When there are a lot of old people in a room, then there is a feeling that the uninvited guest, death, is also there. Yeats was someone else who lived on and wrote for too long. In old age he went daft with all those séances, though at least he got over the fanciful ideas that he had had as a young man about the existence of fairies. Instead he developed quite a penchant for well-endowed women. At this point Tom interrupted, 'Yes but, despite his ceasing to believe in the fairies, it was the fairies who made him rich and famous.'

The man looked at Tom suspiciously.

'Are you an expert on Yeats?'

'No, I'm just a warehouseman who knows what fairies can do and who likes the poetry of Yeats.'

'And how do you know Molly?' The young woman wanted to know.

'I don't think anyone really knows her,' Tom replied evasively.

So this was literary life! Eventually, though there was no sign of anyone who looked like the oh-so-important Mortimer, they were called to order by Barrington who held up a copy of the book. Its dustjacket showed a woman, presumably Natasha, in a *droshky* and she was nervously looking back to see that she was being pursued across the snowy landscape by a dark horseman. Barrington spoke briefly about her novel, which he said was 'a sure-fire winner' and bound to be acclaimed as the *Dr Zhivago* for the seventies. Then Molly read a fairly ghastly page or two in which Natasha was forced by Merdyakov to watch his homosexual rape of Alexei on Alexei's mother's grave. (It was not a well-chosen reading.) While this was going on, a uniformed man entered and waited while Marcus kissed Molly goodbye before following the man out of the room. Once the reading was over and with Marcus gone, Tom guessed that it was safe to come up to the desk and get his proof copy signed.

'Who should I sign this book to?'

Tom said nothing, so she wrote, 'To Tom, the Bard of Cashel.'

A little later the wine ran out and consequently the party started to disperse. As Molly was collecting her things before leaving, Tom went up to her again to thank her for the invitation. But before he could do so, Barrington presented her with a letter which had been addressed to her, care of the publishers. Molly looked at the postmark and sighed. She retreated to the corner of the room, dragging Tom with her, before tearing the envelope open. The note was short and, as she read it, her hand went to her mouth.

'It's from Jaimie. He writes that he is coming for me soon. Also that he has bought a gun and I can choose between returning to St Andrews and death.'

'St Andrews or death… difficult choice that… but now there can be a proper car chase.'

'It's not funny. It's not funny at all. Marcus would have seen him off. But that was his chauffeur just then, come to take him to the airport. He is going to be in the States for at least a month. I need protection… one thing I can do is get a gun myself… um, I think I'll get in touch with Ferdie.'

'Ferdie? What's Ferdie got to do with any of this?'

'Nothing, but we have become friends. I loved the way that he produced the rabbit out of the hat. As you know, I just adore conjuring, sleight of hand and con tricks. Since then I have been to see his conjuring act in the upstairs room of a pub and he has promised to score drugs for me anytime I want. I am pretty sure that if I give him the money, he can also score a gun from one of the Notting Hill pushers that he has dealings with. So Jaimie will find me prepared... but then there is the auction of Lancelyn's library at Bonhams in two weeks' time. I really need to be there.'

'Lancelyn?'

'Yes. I told you about him. He was the one I took up with soon after Bernard vanished. I went up to St Andrews with him and stayed in his big house which was full of weird books. Then a little later he went mad and had to be confined. But he must be out now and he is selling his books. He used to be terribly rich, but perhaps he has fallen on hard times. Anyway, it is possible that he will be there to say goodbye to his beloved library and I want to meet him one last time and tell him how sorry I am for everything that has gone wrong. I must see him if I can. If only I can make things right... the trouble is that Jaimie also knew him very well and he may find a way of getting down from Scotland, either to meet with Lancelyn or guessing to find me at Bonhams and bully me at gunpoint to going back to St Andrews with him... you couldn't... would you come with me to Bonhams as my escort to make sure that nothing happens?'

'When?'

'Viewing is on the Saturday and the actual sale on the Monday, 14 December.'

'I can do the Saturday, but not the Monday.'

'Thank you. Maybe I can get someone else to come along to the sale on the Monday. But give me your phone number so that we can finalise arrangements.'

So now he had a new role to add to those of poet and warehouseman. He was to become a bodyguard. If only he had not gone to that launch... Blaise Pascal wrote that 'all of humanity's problems stem from man's inability to sit quietly in a room alone'. Now an auction loomed. It was another adventure, admittedly again a very small one.

CHAPTER SEVEN

On the Saturday of the viewing they met in Harrods Food Hall. Molly, who was dressed in a black cat suit, attracted a lot of attention. She looked like a more flamboyant version of Mrs Emma Peel in the TV series, *The Avengers*. Tom just wished that he was wearing a suit and bowler hat to go with her. It was only a short walk from Harrods to Bonhams in Montpelier Street. Once inside, Molly walked cautiously round the shelves to check who else might be there, before instructing Tom not to go far and then going off to talk to one of the staff of the auction house. It was an animated conversation and Tom guessed that they might be comparing auction house notes.

Tom hoped Molly would get around to introducing him to the Bonham's staff as her 'minder'. He wandered between the shelves trying to get a sense of what was so special about the library of Lancelyn Delderfield. Though there were no Gutenberg Bibles or Shakespeare First Folios to be seen, there were certainly many rare and strange books: a Japanese treatise on competitive farting; the Comte de St. Germain's *How to Win at Cards*; *Around Russia on Roller Skates*; *Tattooed Fish*; *Tattooed Mountain Women and Wooden Spoon Boxes of Daghestan*; *Mad Artists and Tattooed Perverts*; *The*

Protocols of the Elders of Zion; *Masonic Eyebrow Plucking*; *A Handbook to Poisonous Wallpaper*; *The Holy Prepuce, The Foreskins of Christ, How Multiplied Defended*. In addition to these curiosities there was rather a lot of pornography. Cumulatively the effect was distinctly creepy. It was as if Mr Lancelyn Delderfield was standing close beside and Tom could hear him hoarsely breathing. The creepiness was accentuated by those who had turned up to view the books. From eavesdropping Tom gathered that some were bookdealers who had been familiar with Lancelyn's expensive and exotic tastes. Other sleazy-looking types looked as though they were here for the porn, but maybe they were bookdealers too. He fancied that dispersing the sinister library would be akin to a grand exorcism. He picked a book off the shelf, attracted by its strange title, *What Rough Beast? A Biographical Fantasia on the Life of Professor J. R. Neave, otherwise Known as Iron Foot Jack*, by Mark Benney. A man standing beside Tom said, 'Lancelyn knew Iron Foot Jack. At least they met once in a London coffee bar called *Le Macabre* and Lancelyn told me what a powerful effect that smelly and rather batty character had upon him. Iron Foot Jack came to haunt his dreams.'

'So you knew Delderfield?'

'Yes, I am Quentin Mallow. I teach history in the University of St Andrews. Look at this.'

Quentin, who looked like a slightly younger and slimmer version of Mr Pickwick, showed Tom the book he was holding and said, 'This is unusual. It is an example of anthropodermic bibliopegy.'

Tom could make nothing of this, but said, 'I'm Tom Byrne. I'm here as Molly Ransom's minder.'

'Oh God! Molly is here! How? Why?'

'She thought that Lancelyn might turn up to say goodbye to his books.'

'No, that is not going to happen. Lancelyn is on his yacht, somewhere in the Indian Ocean, the South Seas, or somewhere like that.'

'You also knew Molly?'

'I met her just the once, the first time she came up to St Andrews with her husband. There was a séance at which she was sitting next to Lancelyn and I was sitting next to her and I could see that she had his flies unzipped and was stroking his penis. The séance ended with what seemed to be a curse aimed at Lancelyn. God knows what was going on that evening. Not long after that her husband disappeared. And God knows what happened the second time she came to St Andrews. Since she had lost her husband, Lancelyn brought her back to live with him. But then an oddball character in the English Department started visiting and a kind of *ménage à trois* was established in which Lancelyn was definitely the *troisième,* or even the gooseberry. I don't know the details. I didn't visit the house while whatever was going on was going on and I just heard rumours. But then one morning he came up to me while I was in the staff common room and he had a glove puppet on one hand and a large can of paraffin in the other. He was going to set fire to something or somebody, whether it was the staff common room, or Molly and her lover, or himself, or his books, I don't know. I rang for medical help and he was taken to a mental hospital in Dundee. As you see, his library has been preserved for the doubtful benefit of humanity. But he was my friend — still is. We correspond occasionally when he finds himself on the same continent as me.'

'Molly's lover, the lecturer, was called Jaimie.'

'That's right. If you are with Molly, I should warn you that… but here she comes now, the *Belle Dame Sans Merci*. Forgive me, but it is time for me to scarper. '

Molly came up to Tom. She was smiling and did not seem to have noticed the disappearing Quentin. She was carrying two books. The first of these was *Notorious Impostures of Spiritual Manifestations in Coal Mines Exposed and Their Perpetrators Named, to which is added an Explanation of the Composition of Marsh Gas* (1803).

'Marcus and I were history students together at Oxford and as a student he began collecting books on coal mining simply because they were all so cheap. Then, after he married, his bitch wife made him get rid of them. But more recently he has been rebuilding his collection. It is as if he is looking for the person he once was and trying to rebuild his youth. So I am going to put in a bid for this one. Even something as old and rare as this should not go for much, since rare books on coal mining are still amazingly cheap. Oh — and I asked the man on the desk if there were any books on warehousing and he led me to this.'

She showed Tom the second book, *The Eccentric and extraordinary history of Nath Bentley, Esq., together with an accurate description of his singular habitation usually denominated the dirty warehouse in Leadenhall Street, with many curious and original anecdotes, never before published, to which is prefaced the strange and eccentric life and adventure of Lord Rokeby, whose general propensity was living in water*. The book had no publication date.

Tom wondered if what Lancelyn had really been into was collecting books with long titles. He shook his head and said, 'I am such a slow reader that it would take me a couple of days to get through the title.'

'Oh look, Ferdie has got here after all.'

Molly put the books aside. Ferdie was carrying a tote bag which swung heavily from his shoulder. Tom was guessing that its heavy contents consisted of a pistol and boxes of ammunition.

'Hi, it's good to see you two again,' said Ferdie. 'You have been much missed in the group, especially since you have been replaced by a married couple called Bob and Elsie. The new people are not so interesting and I guess that they have signed up with the group because they are so bored with each other. Also Leon is beginning to look rather gaunt and he is not saying much. Josephine believes that Tom really is a police spy and you are a witch. I had one of those silly sword fights with Raymond, but then it turned into a real fight and we had to be pulled apart. Now I think about it, it is boredom more than anything else that makes people join Quaesitor and there they get to meet people who are just as bored as they are. It is not a solution to anything.'

'I am through with encountering,' said Molly. 'But let me show you some books that are just up your street. She showed him the relevant page in the catalogue. The books in question were Thomas Hill's *A brief and pleasaunt treatise, entitled Naturall and Artificiall Conclusions*, Reginald Scot's *The discoverie of witchcraft*, S. R.'s *The Art of Juggling or Legerdemaine* and the anonymous *Mathematical Recreations*.

Ferdie looked at the entries and shook his head regretfully.

'I could not get near their reserve prices.'

'Ah well,' said Molly. 'But now we have something else to talk about.' Then turning to Tom, she continued, 'You can go now if you want. Now that Ferdie is here, I shall be quite safe. I have your phone number, don't I?'

So that was it. His brief career as a minder seemed to be over. It was a sunny day and he would walk back to Battersea. After those small adventures, Tom decided that he had had enough and that he would devote himself to a study of boredom. He would seek it out in station waiting rooms, empty churches and industrial estates. He would buy a can of paint, slosh some of it on one of his walls and watch it dry. He would set up unvarying routines. He would try to always think about those routines in the same way and would be careful to note when he achieved this that he 'always thought like that'. But yet he feared that at the end of it he would discover what he already knew — that, as someone once remarked, boredom was precisely 'the desire to feel desires'. Eventually Tom got around to looking up 'anthropodermic bibliopegy'. It referred to the practice of binding books in human skin.

> '*Here comes Medea.*
> *Why is she here?*
> *We have no idea.*'

Tom certainly had no idea. Also, what rhymed with Colchis, apart from poultice? Should *The Modern Medea* be in modern dress? Also, since Colchis was so difficult to rhyme with, perhaps his play should be set in London. But what rhymed with London, apart from dum-dum, as in bullets? At the moment he was envisaging the main events as taking place off stage. So, for example, one would only hear of the murder of the children by report. Medea would usually be centre stage, but behind her would be a chorus of twelve, rejoicing or lamenting at what Medea narrated, mostly lamenting. But the chorus also offers her co-counselling. However she warns them not to approach her and says she is not going to listen to them. The King of Colchis (who, in Tom's head, looked just like Philip) sat a little apart. Maybe the children heard being murdered offstage were Janet's children. Anything was possible. Indeed, far too much was possible. That was the problem. Also he ought to be more ambitious and think beyond the stage play and look to the play's future in the cinema. He ought to make his drama filmic. A car chase or a shootout in a deserted warehouse might be cinematic.

Tom wondered if Molly had made a start on her next novel and, if so, how she was getting on with it. He would lay even money that it was going to be about Mary Queen of Scots. If that was the case, he stood a faint chance of featuring in her book as Bothwell or Rizzio, but really it was more likely he would only be in the service of the drama queen as 'an attendant lord' (as T. S. Eliot would have put it). Tom reckoned that there was not enough of him to be a suitable subject for a novel. Mary would be ravishing, impetuous, arrogant, passionate and fond of dancing. But rather unlucky in love. She and her lovers would be doing whatever the Tudor version of kinky sex was. Also there would be the galliard and the volta. Vivacious Mary would be surrounded by Puritan peers dressed in black. Angry but courteous men with swords would clash with one another.

Never mind all that. Should Medea be presented as victim

or victor? Should she murder her children as in the plays and legends? At what point should her story start? Was Medea ever an innocent little girl? Had Molly had any children? She was perhaps a kind of praying mantis, or should that be preying mantis? Anyway the mantis that bites her husband's head off. When the play opens the plague has fallen on Colchis or London? Anyway the plague had to be exorcised and sin expiated. What sort of metre should his play be in? Could it be free verse? What was the point of rhyme? Was there any percentage in having the chorus in the nude? Probably not. How would Yeats have managed with *The New Medea*? Faced with any problem, he should always turn to Yeats. What would Yeats do in a car chase, or when faced by a gun-toting stalker? Come to that, how good would he have been as a warehouse manager? Perhaps, after all, it was time to move away from Yeats. Nothing really rhymed with Colchis, not properly. Maybe he could get away with bogus, lotus or atrocious. Atrocious might be useful. The other thing he had to bear in mind was that *The Modern Medea* had to have contemporary relevance. It ought to be about American imperialism, the feminist movement, the dangers of drug-taking, Rhodesia's declaration of U.D.I. or *something*. Above all *The Modern Medea* had to be relevant to modern men and women.

A play should have a beginning, a middle and an end. That seemed to be the consensus.

Then the phone rang. It was Molly, 'Tom, are you free next Saturday? How would you like a trip to Oxford? I will cover all your expenses, if you can accompany me. Oxford is ever so beautiful, if you have never been there.'

'What is going on, Molly?'

'It is Bernard's and Lancelyn's old English Literature tutor, Edward Raven. He has been senile and in a care home for goodness knows how many years. Now he has died and I ought to attend his funeral. We were good friends and besides there is a chance that Lancelyn might be there and I really really want to pay penance to him. But Marcus is still in the States. He keeps ringing to tell me that his business is keeping him there longer than he expected. I wouldn't be surprised if the 'business' wasn't some hooker, but that's not the point. I'm fearful that Jaimie might follow me to the funeral. I really would welcome your company. Please.'

'So I'm to be reinstated as your bodyguard?'

'Er… yes please.'

'So Jaimie has a gun and you are hoping that I might be able to step in the way and take the bullet that was meant for you.'

'No. No, it wouldn't be like that. I don't think that he wants to kill me, but he might well use it in a kidnap attempt.'

Tom was silent a long time. He was trying to imagine the possible kidnap scene at Paddington Station or in an Oxford cemetery. Back on the Carousel of Adventure?

Molly had to ask, 'Are you still there? Tom, please.'

'Very well. I'll come.'

'Thank you, thank you. I will tell you about Raven on the way up. He was quite a character. And I can show you some of the sights of the city after the funeral.'

CHAPTER EIGHT

They met at Paddington Station. Molly, in high-heeled black boots, was wearing a black jacket, white blouse, calf-length skirt, a silver belt and the broad-brimmed black hat. She proudly showed him the big new handbag that she had bought to go with her outfit. On the train, as promised she started to talk about Oxford and Edward Raven.

'I was so innocent when I came up to Oxford. All I knew was that I wanted to write novels. Then I met Bernard and Lancelyn, two brilliant English Literature undergraduates. They were both mad about crosswords, by the way. Take it from me, cryptic crosswords are not only a massive waste of time, but they twist the minds of those who do them, so that they come to see life as a gigantic rebus. Finding hidden significances in crossword clues is one thing, but finding hidden significance in everyday events in the real world is another, for that way madness lies. Poor Lancelyn! He was so handsome and clever and so lost — and so frightened of me! When Bernard and I went up to St Andrews to visit Lancelyn, I could see that he was worried about something and I tried to cheer him up. Bernard did not like that. But I am getting ahead of myself and I don't want to talk about what happened in St Andrews. It is Raven I want to talk about. Though I really fancied Lancelyn, I ended up going out with Bernard. Then at the end of their last final's paper I met them outside the Examination Schools. Their brilliant and enigmatic tutor, Raven was there with bottles of champagne. I was carrying a copy of *The Times* with me and, after some preliminary chat, Lancelyn snatched the paper from me and he and Bernard settled down with their champagne to do the crossword. So I found myself having a conversation with Raven. I had never met him before, but we got on really well and then we kept running into one another in town. Eventually he started inviting me out to lunch. I thought it might be a prelude to him making a pass at me. It is hard work being beautiful. But, no, he behaved like a perfect gentleman. He liked to hear my gossip and in particular I think he wanted to use me to keep tabs on his most recent star pupils. I think that he had some grand project in which he hoped to get them involved. I don't know. Bernard and Lancelyn revered him, because during the Second World War the Italian Resistance had managed to find him a hiding place in a monastery in the mountains where he not only found God but also discovered a new way of teaching English Literature called the Ignatian technique. I am not the one to ask about that.

'It was only a year or so later, after Bernard had disappeared and Raven's dementia was beginning to set in, when Lancelyn turned up in Oxford and confronted him with the truth, which was that he had never fought in Italy and that he had spent most of the war years in prison as a convicted paedophile. He did not attempt to deny this and it was also at this confrontation that I learnt from Raven that it was Lancelyn who had written *The Times Literary Supplement* killer review which had destroyed Bernard's academic reputation and may have led to his disappearance. After that confrontation, Lancelyn took me back with him to St Andrews. It was obvious he was distressed. I thought it was because of his recent discovery of the truth about Raven and then finding that Raven was going senile. I don't know how much of all this makes sense to you. I can't entirely make sense of it myself. But that was all so long ago and I'm sure that you don't want or need to know about it. It is all past and finished with. All the same life became so dull when first Bernard and then Lancelyn vanished and Raven was put in a care home.'

It was all so vivid to her, but to Tom it was just a confused story about people he would never encounter. It was like being told about a wonderful film which was no longer on release. Molly was excited at the prospect that 'poor Lancelyn' might turn up at Raven's funeral. Excited, but also somewhat fearful. Tom had not said anything about his encounter with Quentin Mallow and how he knew it was wildly unlikely that Lancelyn would be there. Then Molly started on about how angry she was that so far *The Rod and the Knout* had had no reviews. When she dozed off a little before Didcot, Tom surreptitiously lifted the heavy handbag. Yes that would be the gun.

Pachelbel's *Canon in D* was playing as they entered the church. A priest was standing at the altar and beside him was a handsome man with a crewcut wearing a smartly tailored dark mohair Burberry suit. Also leather gloves. Obviously American. After the organ music finished there was a long silence. Then the American reached behind the altar and brought up an old Grundig tape recorder which he plonked on the altar. He surveyed the congregation carefully before beginning his address.

'I flew in yesterday to be here for Edward Raven's funeral and for me at least it is strangely appropriate to be addressing you in the Church of Saint Joseph of Cupertino, since, as I am sure you are aware, he is the patron saint of air travellers. I am Colonel Charles Bolton, based at the Pentagon, reporting here for a most melancholy duty. I was a Rhodes Scholar here in Oxford in the late fifties. Of course, I am proud to have been a Rhodes Scholar, but I am even more proud to have been one of the chosen elite among Mr. Edward Raven's students and, by the way, I can see at least two others from that privileged body who are in the congregation this morning, Edward Sanderson from the Frankfurt Central Bank and Mortimer Salter from *The Times Literary Supplement*. This is not the place to go into any detail on the Ignatian method. It has to be experienced at first hand rather than learnt about by report. But briefly it is a technique of visualisation and total immersion in a chosen passage of literature which Raven modelled upon the seventeenth-century *Spiritual Exercises of St Ignatius of Loyola*. Ignatius held that through coming close to the sufferings of Christ, one may be led to salvation. During the Second World War Raven was a combatant who took part in the Allied landings. Later when he was cut off from his unit, he was helped by members of the Resistance to find safety in a monastery in the Apennines and it was there that he found Christian peace and discovered the wisdom of St. Ignatius.'

At this point Molly and Tom looked at one another.

'Oh dear!' whispered Molly.

The Colonel continued, 'Applied to the study of literature,

Raven's Ignatian method gets results. I would go further, for I have used this technique better to understand combat reports and I have even got a class to study the Tet Offensive using the Ignatian exercises. But I am not here to talk about myself. As most of you will know, Raven was eventually afflicted with severe dementia and he spent his last years being looked after in a care home. However, when he had the diagnosis of incipient dementia first confirmed to him, he took steps to ensure that his grand project should outlive him and so, while he was still able to muster his thoughts on this crucial matter, he made two tape recordings which he entrusted to me.'

The Colonel then turned to the tape recorder and switched it on.

First there was a song from *Porgy and Bess*, the refrain of which ran as follows:

> '*It ain't necessarily so*
> *That what you're liable*
> *To read in the Bible,*
> *It ain't necessarily so.*'

The Colonel looked disconcerted and muttered, 'His little joke. He was, as you will all know an intensely pious man. Indeed I should say that he was God obsessed…

Then another voice cut in, 'Good day to you all and thank you for being here. This is Edward Raven speaking to you from beyond the grave — at least, if I am not actually in it, I guess that I very soon will be. Of late I have noticed the beginning of a certain decline in my mental faculties and I therefore thought that, while there was still time, I should outline the underlying idea behind my ambitious project, particularly to those who wittingly or unwittingly have found themselves to be part of that project. I don't know how the details of that are working out, but I hope that Molly, Ed... Mortimer, Lancelyn, and... er, Bernard and... er, one or two others may be present.

'From what the doctors have told me, they believe that my story may be coming to an end. Naturally I am opposed to this, for in my case it seems premature, since there are many loose ends in my story that have yet to be tidied up and, inevitably, my story overlaps with the stories of others who... are destined to outlive me. If memory serves... though my memory is not such a good servant as it used to be... if memory serves, somewhere, in an obscurely published article, the Bulgarian literary theorist Tzvetan Todorov argues that the narrative of *The Quest of the Holy Grail* is really the story of the quest for the story of the quest for the Holy Grail. It is the quest for its own narrative. So where do I go from there?... hum... I believe that, as in literature, so it is in life.

'Secondly, *The Quest of the Holy Grail* strikes me as, in a way, vaguely similar to your common-or-garden murder mystery in which the detective's quest is to unfold the story of the murder, the story of how it was committed by whom, how and when. But that is by the way. Oh dear, where am I going with this... oh yes. Certain people's lives follow plots, just as in novels, and, just as in novels, life has its clichés, repetitions and inconsistencies. Also retardation, defamiliarisation and delayed decoding. Most lives are like poor dreams, drifting on from one damn thing to another. For the chosen few, however, for those who will have stories, it will be different and any repetitions, inconsistencies and suchlike in their lives will be in the service of art. I have wished to go beyond teaching literature and I have desired to make literature happen in real life. So my project was and will be to use real people to inhabit and make their own stories. So now, what is a story? Oh dear, I did once know the answer to that. Never mind… what I think I want to say here is that, with a story that is happening in reality, this story should not just entertain the onlookers, but also the protagonists who are making the story happen. They will be like dancers:

> "*O body swayed by music, O brightening glance,*
> *How can we tell the dancer from the dance?*"'

Suddenly Tom, who had been sitting slumped, sat bolt upright. That was Yeats! That was 'Among School Children'! Raven continued, 'I am afraid that I have lost my thread. I suppose that any old thread will do. But not if I have lost it. While I am thinking what my thread was, let me tell you about Homer's *Iliad*. Yes, that was going to be the first thing I wanted to talk about. This epic story does not open with the Judgement of Paris, nor with his abduction of Helen, nor with the launching of the Greek fleet against Troy, nor even with the commencement of the siege of that city, but with Agamemnon's taking of the slave — Briseis was her name if I remember rightly — from Achilles, and thereafter the story continues with the consequences of the anger of Achilles. But then the story does not go on to end with the construction of the wooden horse, the sacking of Troy and the subsequent return of the Greek heroes to their various islands and cities. It ends much earlier with the slaying of Hector by Achilles. So almost everything that is important to the story happens outside the story. This has got little or nothing to do with what I wanted to tell you. Which I have now remembered…

'You may think my project arrogant and foolish and that I am playing God. In a way, so I am — just as small children may play at being bus conductors or nurses under the watchful eye of their parent. I'm getting tired and need to bring this to a close as soon as possible. The one big thing I learnt from my sojourn in the Italian monastery is that a proper story has to receive God's good grace and sanction. According to a Hassidic saying, "the soul teaches but it never repeats itself". A well-made story has to have an end and a point. It is the task of my… my chosen few to discover what the story is. You, the chosen few, will be like readers, except you are the characters you are reading about. What else? Yes… even after the book has been finished, it may live on in the mind of the reader and of course sequels are not unknown. For my chosen few, their task is to immerse themselves in their own stories until they come fully to understand what those stories are. The days and nights will spin round like pages being turned in a book. You come from God and to him you must return. The second tape should make things clearer.'

Then there was the sound of the tape spinning loose on its spool. Tom waited for the second tape to be played, but this did not happen. Instead the tape recorder was removed from the altar and the priest addressed the congregation with some conventional pieties and all-purpose remarks about the deceased. The coffin was carried out and there was more organ music, before, after an appropriate interval, the congregation proceeded out to the cemetery. Outside it was damp, almost amounting to drizzle. As the pallbearers were lowering the coffin into the grave, Tom had the absurd fantasy that the second tape might be inside the coffin and that they might hear Raven's voice exhorting the pallbearers, 'Easy does it! Take it gently now!'

But the coffin was silently lowered into its resting place.

As so often, Yeats was in Tom's head:

> *'Cast a cold eye*
> *On life, on death.*
> *Horseman pass by!'*

The Colonel threw the first clod of earth onto the coffin. At that moment Molly pointed towards the church's lychgate and screamed. There was, Tom thought, a man standing in its shadows, though only his pale face was properly visible and he looked as terrified as Molly was.

Molly teetered forward and was in danger of falling into the grave, but Tom pulled her back in time. By then the white face had vanished.

'Is that Jaimie?'

'No way. It was Bernard, or his ghost.'

(Which one was Bernard? Oh yes.)

Now she was quietly weeping.

'You saw him too?'

'I saw a face.'

'Silly of me. It can't really have been Bernard, but his face was so like Bernard's was so many years ago.'

CHAPTER NINE

Merton was only a short walk away and light refreshments were now going to be served in its Common Room. Tom decided that he did not want to be making conversational heavy weather with a lot of academics and that he would prefer a beer and a scotch egg in a pub. So he arranged to meet Molly again in the porter's lodge in an hour and a half's time. It was a short walk to The Chequers on the High Street and the first thing he saw when he entered the pub was Bernard or his ghost sitting at a table with a plate of steak pie and chips and a pint of beer. So Tom went up to him and said, 'You're Bernard, aren't you?'

'Who are you and how do you know my name?'

'My name is Tom Byrne and I am Molly's bodyguard.'

'Bodyguard eh? When I was last with her she was just a housewife. Now she has a bodyguard.' He shrugged. 'What does she need a bodyguard for?'

'There is a man who has been stalking her and he has a gun.'

Bernard shrugged again, 'Good luck to him.'

'Molly saw you. She thought you were a ghost.'

Bernard smiled sadly.

'Perhaps I am, in a way. This very table was where I and my friend Lancelyn first met Molly so many years ago. Now, I did not think that there would be anyone at the funeral that I knew, except maybe Lancelyn. How is my beloved wife? No, don't bother to answer that. I'm not interested. She looked older. Shadows under her eyes.'

'She thought you were dead. She has had you registered as dead.'

'Is that so? Well, it's more fun being dead than you might imagine.'

'Where have you been? What have you been doing? Why are you here?'

'Buy me a beer and I will tell you. My story is a strange one.'

Tom bought two beers, plus a steak pie and chips for himself and then the strange story could commence, 'It was ten years ago or so. It almost seems like yesterday. I was so desperate that I thought I might top myself. My academic career, which had had such a brilliant start, seemed to be in tatters. My book, *Towards a Reinvention of Edwardian Fictionality: Deconstructing the Hegemonic Ghost Stories of M. R. James*, had received a slaughterous review in *The Times Literary Supplement*. It was looking unlikely that my research fellowship would be extended. And Molly did not take to domesticity easily. She was always extravagant and clothes mad. Also a terrible cook with a low boredom threshold. Then, on a trip to Scotland, she insisted on sleeping with Lancelyn, who was my best friend, and, later, when we got back to Oxford, she told me that she was thinking of leaving me. I don't blame Lancelyn, by the way. He was never the one to

77

initiate anything with women.

'Anyway, I had just got around to considering where I could attach a strong rope when there was a knocking on the door of my study in All Souls. It was a young American woman called Cassandra. She was pretty with an elfin face and short blonde hair like a golden helmet. She apologised for dropping by without an appointment, but she had been driving through Oxford on her way back to the Institute and she thought that she should look in on the off-chance, since she had a research job to offer me. *Towards a Reinvention of Edwardian Fictionality* had made a great impression on the people in her organisation and they were looking for someone who was an expert, or, better yet, *the* expert on ghost stories to join in the Institute's project. The Bradbury Institute, which was newly established in Newcastle, was prepared to pay well. It was five thousand a month! But then she said that she knew that this was all a long shot and that I was probably tied up with all sorts of things. I sat there thinking about the rope that I had been planning to buy. Then I asked her when would they want me to start? She said as soon as possible, as soon as I was ready.

'I just sat there for another ten or fifteen minutes thinking. Then I said that I was almost ready to start right now. I would just need to collect some things from the cottage. She took this pretty calmly, though she was obviously pleased and she said that she had her car parked in Broad Street and that she could drive me to the cottage before we drove on to Newcastle. So I collected a pile of books and walked out with her to Broad Street. I knew Molly would be out having one of her lunches with the don called Raven. So, once in the cottage, I filled a suitcase with some clothes and some books and found my passport and then we set out for Newcastle.

'During the drive I was keen to talk about the research project and what my part in it would be. But she said that all that would best be done at the Institute with the relevant papers, instruments and the other researchers present. Instead it would be nice, as she drove, if we got to know one another.

'I didn't say much about my family life. Mostly I talked about my time in Oxford and how much I had wanted to be a member of the Bullingdon Club and how I met Lancelyn and how he taught me to talk and behave like someone who had been to public school. (He'd been to Eton, you know.) And about Raven's English Literature tutorials and how he taught us a way of entering into classic works of literature using a visualisation technique that was based on *The Spiritual Exercises of St Ignatius of Loyola*. Consequently we both got firsts, but…'

'Was Lancelyn showing any signs of insanity as a student or afterwards?'

'Lancelyn? No none at all… unless sleeping with Molly counts as a form of insanity. Anyway, as I was saying, before we had taken our degrees, we both had that ill-fated encounter with Molly and, as I say, in this very pub.

'Though it was a long drive, it was mostly me talking about myself. Cassandra did not say so much about herself. She soon told me to call her Cassie.

'The Bradbury Institute is in Newcastle's Mayflower Road. There was great excitement at my arrival and very quickly a late-evening feast was knocked together. The food was rather weird and I'll come back to that. The Institute's staff consisted of nine young women, including Cassie, and an aged caretaker, but he did not eat with us. There was plenty to drink and I was soon happy to be shown my bedroom. The briefing would be held on the following morning. I slept heavily and in the morning had some difficulty remembering where I was at first. I dressed and followed my nose to breakfast. The briefing began half an hour after that.

'It took place in what I came to think of as the boardroom. My fellow researchers were all American women: one astrophysicist, two astronomers, a psychical researcher, an archaeologist, a palaeontologist, a chemical analyst, a data analyst and Cassie who was in charge of admin. So I was the only person who knew about ghost stories and traditional ghost lore. Then the first thing that occurred to me was how come they were all women? I was told that the men, who were based in the States, were into the "boys' toys stuff", such as the calculation of orbital velocities, the composition of booster fuels, and fitness programmes for astronauts. It was only at this point that I was informed that the Bradbury Institute was a branch of NASA, the National Aeronautics and Space Administration. I was still digesting this when the palaeontologist took me through the sort of stuff she specialised in. "Palaeontologist" was a layman's term, a simplification of what she actually was an expert on. Whereas your run-of-the-mill palaeontologist specialised in ammonites, dinosaurs, woolly mammoths, those kind of things, she specialised in what are known as ichnites, that is, not the dinosaurs, but the traces left by the dinosaurs, which are usually footprints. She spent some time on this palaeoichnites stuff and I was still taking it in when a big map of Mars showing its massive craters and crevasses came up on the screen behind me and the astronomer took me though the leading features of the planet's topography. Olympus Mons was a volcanic mountain fifteen miles high, the largest volcano in the solar system. Valles Marineris was a great canyon which extended for three thousand miles. I was shown the barchans, vast crescent-shaped sand dunes which, driven by fierce winds, rolled across the planet, and so many other geological wonders.

'Then it was the turn of the archaeologist to explain that no traces of Martian habitations had been observed. Well, even I knew that. Nevertheless, it did seem more likely than not that the planet had once been habitable. The planet has carbon, hydrogen, oxygen, phosphorus and sulphur. Four billion years ago Mars had been warm and wet. So life there was not only possible, but almost inevitable. Now came the crunch. It was evident that no Martians had survived and, if they had ever existed, they would have been dead for centuries or even millennia, but... but... but it was possible that the planet was haunted and that the Martians had survived as a form of afterlife. Though it was hardly likely, it was still a remote possibility that had to be investigated and indeed there were indications that the Russians were also researching this possibility. So the Institute wanted to use my extensive knowledge of what our earthly ghosts were supposed to look like and how they behaved, in order to give them some idea of what a Martian ghost might look like and how it would behave. In studying the distant past of Mars, the Institute was also studying the future of Earth, for there will come a time when our planet is inhabited only by ghosts.

'So there it was. I had been headhunted to become Britain's

first palaeo psychographer. All these briefings took a long time and once they had finished we moved on to lunch. Throughout my stay at the Institute, they fed me on strange foods. I looked at the block of white stuff on my plate and had to ask what it was. I was told that it was tofu. Not very nice. In the days and meals that followed I was introduced to cavolo nero, quinoa, kohlrabi, edamame, quark, kori thins, taleggio, limoncello, miso, chermoula, mirin, orzo, amaranth and mung beans. Where was all this stuff coming from? Why were we eating it? Was some or all of it hallucinogenic? I had a wonderful time at the Institute, except, that is, for those infernal lunches and dinners. I used to envy that castaway in *Treasure Island*, Ben Gunn, who dreamt of toasted cheese, whereas I mostly had anxiety dreams about tofu and quinoa. But that is by the way. In the afternoon I was shown to my office and there I made a start on listing the books and articles that I would need in addition to the ones I had brought with me. I was told that there would be no problem in getting hold of anything I needed. The stuff they already had was very old and not terribly useful, stuff like Emmanuel Swedenborg's *De Telluribus in Mundo Nostro Solari* (1758) and Theodor Flournoy's *From India to the Planet Mars* (1899) which recorded alleged séances with Martians that had been held between 1894 and 1901. No use at all.

'In the evening, there was dancing. I had never learned to dance, but Cassie insisted on taking me in hand. There was a cassette player — something that I had never seen before — and we danced to all manner of tunes, but mostly Irish jigs and Highland dances, I think. Apart from the caretaker, I was the only man in the Institute. So they all wanted to dance with

82

me and I was flung from one young woman to the next. The tunes came round and round and we danced like waves in the sea. The caretaker's knees were too arthritic for dancing, but he sometimes liked to watch. Those were my dancing years. There were dances usually three or four times a week. Eventually my shoes wore out and a shoemaker had to be sent for. This little old man with spectacles on his pointed nose was the only stranger that I ever saw admitted to the Institute during my time there. He measured my feet, whistling as he did so, and three days later he returned with the new shoes. They were, as he said, quite wonderful for dancing.

'Apart from dancing, the women liked to sit in a circle and tell stories. It was supposed to be good for the mind. I heard all manner of strange tales. As for myself, at first I put my undergraduate studies in English Literature to good use and I told them stories from Stevenson, Conan Doyle, Conrad and, above all, the ghost stories of M. R. James, but eventually I decided to tell my own sad story of how I had lost my way in academia and been betrayed by my wife with my best friend and how close I had come to the abyss when Cassie came knocking on my door. They all cooed over me and Cassie was extra tender with me that night… oh, I forgot to mention that Cassie came to my bed on the second night of my stay at the Institute and thereafter the researchers took turns in coming to my room. This was all so different from All Souls.'

Bernard pointed to his empty beer mug. Tom fetched him another pint and then resumed his musing. Was the man an idiot, a lunatic, or a compulsive liar? Bernard continued, 'Though there was a television in the Institute, it was rarely switched on, except for coverage of NASA's rocket launches in Project Gemini and Project Mercury and the successive Mariner explorations… oh, and they loved watching *Star Trek*. I quite enjoyed that series too and they used to tease me about how I fancied the black female officer Uhura and her beautiful legs. Well, I did. I never left the Institute, except for short walks in a park nearby. The Institute had a sunroof on which a powerful telescope had been installed and, weather permitting, I liked to work there. Occasionally I trained the telescope on the street below and tried to imagine what living in Newcastle might be like, outside the Institute, that is. But it was enough to imagine this. I had no desire to find out what this might really be like. My allotted task was, of course, extremely difficult. In the past, there had been a tendency to project earth-born fantasies onto Mars — witness the *Flash Gordon* films, the novels of Edgar Rice Burroughs and the *Dan Dare* cartoon strips. We had to clear our minds of such nonsense. As it was — or at least seemed — we were so lonely in our solar system. Even if we had ghostly company, it was unlikely that a Martian ghost would look like a human ghost. A Martian spectre might resemble an insect, or a gas, or a puddle of fluid. It might not even manifest itself within the range of human vision. Then what sort of place would it choose to haunt? There was so little to go on that really palaeo psychography was a branch of science with no data at all and so it was a subject for which there might not be an object.

A foreshadowing of doom came with the American landing on the Moon. We sat round the television for hours on end and the viewing was grim. The consensus at the Institute was that the landing had been a big mistake. When Neil Armstrong went clumping about on its surface in his big heavy boots, he destroyed the mystery and romance of the Moon forever. We could only hope and pray that Mars would not fall prey to the same disaster. It seemed obvious to us that it was much better to study Mars from a distance.

'Despite the lack of progress, I was happy in my researches. Only those strange foods were getting me down. After one hard morning's work, I realised that what I really fancied for lunch was some good old-fashioned fish and chips. So I slipped out of the Institute and went round the corner and bought some battered fish with chips wrapped in a newspaper and took it to a bench in the park to eat. It was heavenly. I thought that it might be the best meal that I had ever tasted in my life, or ever would. Then my eye caught the date on the top of newspaper's page. I had had no idea at all that so much time had passed. An even bigger shock awaited me when I got back to the Institute. First, I had trouble getting back in, though eventually Cassie answered the door and let me enter. "Oh there you are. We have packed your stuff up for you to take away. I will go and find what I'm afraid will be your last lot of money." There was a lot of noise throughout the Institute and the women were busy rolling up maps, wrapping instruments in straw and putting things in crates. Eventually Cassie found time to explain that NASA had unexpectedly suffered a shortfall in funding and consequently it was having to shut down the Institute in Britain and recall its staff back to the States. Maybe it was a temporary economy. All the same, we had not been making much progress had we? That was what she said, but I think it may have been their lack of enthusiasm for the Moon landing that did for them. I noticed, now that the packing was underway, the caretaker, who was standing straighter, was in charge. Perhaps he always had been. My stuff was all in two suitcases, the second of which was new and was for the extra books. Before the door closed on me, Cassie said that she would write. But how could she? She could have no idea where I am now, or where I may be living next week. Now, how does one get a job as a bodyguard?'

'Sorry, I have no idea. I have only amateur status as one. Molly just asked me to accompany her to the funeral because she was afraid that she was being stalked by a man with a gun.'

'That's a pity. I was hoping you could point me to a bodyguarding agency in London or elsewhere. I have come down to Oxford in the faint hope that either All Souls or Merton would have something for me. Faint hope! If only I had succeeded in getting into the Bullingdon Club, they might have helped me. Then I heard about Raven's funeral and I thought that I would go along, partly to pay my respects to the great teacher, but also in the hope of finding Lancelyn there. I did not think about Molly. Anyway, to round off my strange story, after the Institute closed its doors on me, I booked myself into a Newcastle bed-and-breakfast and then spent three days visiting all the shoe shops and shoemakers in the city that I could locate, yet no one I talked to could identify the shoemaker I described, though many of them did admire the shoes I was wearing. An exceptionally professional job, they said. By the way, I have no idea why I was looking for the shoemaker, except that I was out of my mind with grief. Since then my shoes have taken me criss-crossing England in a hunt for work. One would have thought that a starred first at Oxford counted for something... though I left the Institute with lots of money, it will eventually run out. I think that next I might go down to London and try the Society for Psychical Research. It is either them or giving dancing lessons. Well, that's it. That's my story. You won't tell Molly any of this, will you? I don't want her pity. You won't tell her you've seen me?'

Tom shook his head.

'Do you have a strange story that you want to tell me?'

Tom shook his head again, 'Nothing strange ever happens to me. Besides, I am now due back to meet Molly at Merton and then reassume my job as bodyguard.'

'Good luck with that.'

As Tom left the pub, Bernard seemed to be considering another pint. Tom was thinking that the people at the Institute were right. The American landing on the Moon and Neil Armstrong's clumping along through its dust had destroyed the Moon as a subject for poetry as effectively as if the Americans had destroyed the satellite in a series of massive nuclear explosions. It might be that Byron had predicted it:

'Yet we'll go no more a roving
By the light of the moon.'

And, from now on, it would no longer be possible for poets to write, as Yeats had done:

'When have I last looked on
The ground green eyes and the long wavering bodies
Of the dark leopards of the Moon?'

Instead we were stuck with a hunk of useless rock circling overhead. Just as he entered Merton Street Tom swore. It was too late now, but he wished that he had got a good look at Bernard's shoes. He envied Bernard's time in Newcastle. If only Tom could have stumbled across the Bradbury Institute, then perhaps he might have become Martian Poet in Residence. Molly, Bernard, Lancelyn, Raven, Mallow... it seemed to Tom that only Oxbridge types were entitled to adventures. Molly was waiting for him at the porter's lodge. She was very cheerful after the drinks. She introduced him to Colonel Charles Bolton. He and Tom shook hands. Charles was still wearing gloves. Tom wanted to know about the second tape.

'It's in a safe in the Pentagon. It will be played when I judge that we are all ready to hear it.'

Then the Colonel hurried away.

'A charming man. He was telling me about life in the Pentagon.'

The weather was too dismal for proper sightseeing, but, as they made their way to the station, Molly pointed out Corpus, Christ Church and Oxford Castle. She loved Oxford for having been the chosen capital of the Cavaliers, for having been, as Matthew Arnold described it, 'Home of lost causes, and forsaken beliefs, and unpopular names and impossible loyalties'. And Oxford was so medieval! She loved the Middle Ages. She just wanted horrible people like Philip IV out of it.

CHAPTER TEN

As the train pulled out of the station, Molly started talking ten to the dozen about the Colonel and how keen he was to track down Bernard and Lancelyn because they were part of Raven's project. She guessed that she was also part of it and she detested being used in such a fashion.

'Raven talked rubbish like that when Lancelyn and I last visited him. All the same, I feel vaguely menaced by his rubbish. It is as if he has got me in an invisible cage, but I am determined not to be used in this way. I am going to work out what he thinks my story is going to be and then I am going to make a point of disappointing his expectations... I know! I shall become a dinner lady! It will be like Maria Callas deciding to be a traffic warden. Otherwise I would feel that I was being press-ganged into some kind of blasted child's treasure hunt. But I shall not be part of Raven's story and, what's more, I am damned if I am going to be brought by him to God!'

It was some time before Tom could get a word in edgeways and tell her that he had actually had lunch with Bernard. When he had finished, Molly laughed, 'Wow! Those girls sure took him in hand! And he used to be such a boring person! And now he knows how to dance! He got just what he needed. I bet he is a better lover too. What did he say about me?'

Tom decided to leave out the stuff about Molly being high maintenance. So he just said, 'Nothing… except that he never wanted to have anything more to do with you.'

But Molly said that Marcus was wanting to marry her and she was fretting about how Bernard might turn up in the middle of the wedding ceremony and put a stop to it. That would be like that scene in *Jane Eyre* when the brother of the madwoman in the attic turns up during the service and prevents the wedding of Jane and Mr Rochester.

An old man was sitting opposite them reading *Anna Karenina*. Now he looked up and said, 'The brother would be Richard Mason.'

Then he returned to *Anna Karenina*. As he finished each page, he tore it out of the book, put it out of the window and watched it float away in the wind. There was to be no going back for Anna.

Now Molly was wondering if the dramatic scene with Bernard turning up at her wedding might be part of Raven's plot for her. Meanwhile all Tom's suspicions about the expedition to Oxford were coming together and he could be silent no longer, 'Did Jaimie know Raven?'

'No.'

'Did he know anything about Raven?'

'No. I don't think so.'

'So it was not likely that he would turn up at Raven's funeral and you did not really need me as a bodyguard. And, if you wanted a bodyguard, why not Ferdie? So why am I here?'

Molly laughed.

'I thought that you should see Oxford. And Ferdie has an important exam to face today. It's crucial for his career. He has to perform in front of a panel of senior members of the Magic Circle. Ferdie is gay by the way. Hadn't you spotted that?'

(Tom was hopeless at identifying who was gay. How did other people do that?)

'He quite fancies you, by the way.'

But Tom was not so easily diverted.

'You did not need me as a bodyguard, did you?'

Molly smiled.

'No, my desires are otherwise. I just thought that we should get to know one another better.'

'You are mad.'

'No, just a little bored and very lustful. My place or yours?'

And she put her hand on his crotch. (Fortunately the old gentleman was still deeply absorbed in putting an end to *Anna Karenina*.) It was hard for Tom to argue with his second head which was as hard as a skull between his legs. Being desired is a great aphrodisiac. They settled on Highgate. Tom thought that sex with the destroyer of men might count as a big adventure. What kind of doom would follow from this 'shudder in the loins?' Would he end up a thief, an alcoholic, a stalker or a madman? If he got to choose, he would pick alcoholic. Despite the obvious danger, he told himself that screwing her would be necessary research for his verse drama. He did need to sleep with Medea. Probably Flaubert wished that he had slept with Madame Bovary. Ditto Tolstoy with Anna Karenina.

Molly's flat was smartly furnished. There were a number of choice objects on display that might possibly have been picked up cheap at Sotheby's. In the bedroom there was a shelf of books, mostly biographies and popular histories, such as Henrietta Marshall's *Our Island Story* and Antonia Fraser's *Mary Queen of Scots*. His two paperback volumes of poetry were lying face up at the end of the shelf. Molly removed Gladly, her teddy bear from the bed. Gladly? Gladly, the cross-eyed bear. Then she hung her skirt and jacket up in a well-stocked wardrobe before disappearing into the bathroom. Tom took advantage of her absence from the bedroom to feel the pages of his paperbacks. It was clear that the books had not previously been opened.

She was naked when she came back into the bedroom and she was carrying the gun. She placed it firmly in Tom's hand, saying,

'And now you can make me do whatever you want.'

And he did.

A little later when he was in a post-coital doze he suddenly felt something cold pressed against his head.

'Now it's my turn,' she said. 'Now I can make you do whatever I want.'

And she did.

When he awoke he thought he could hear her humming as she made breakfast in the kitchen. It was Sunday. He lay back thinking what they might do. The Zoo? A museum? A walk on Hampstead Heath? Perhaps he should show her round his warehouse? Then she might understand what he had been talking about. When she came back into the room with the breakfast tray, he put the options to her.

'It's no good. The Pentagon man Charles Bolton is giving me lunch at The Ivy. Only a short walk will be possible.

Highgate Cemetery is close. On the other hand, we could just spend the rest of the morning in bed.'

They took the easy option. In the morning light he asked her about the tattoo of a *fleur-de-lis* that he had noticed on her right arm. She told him that it was her badge and a sign of her romantic attachment to the old Bourbon monarchy that had been brought to such a tragically bloody end by the revolutionary *sans-culottes*.

That evening, as arranged, Molly turned up at Tom's flat. Tom thought that he could detect a look of faint dismay on her face as she contemplated the place's austerity. There was no television. The walls were bare except for a reproduction of a copy of Leonardo's '*Leda and the Swan*' by one of his disciples and an engraving of '*Ruins at Cashel*'. He hastily tidied away his working notes on *The New Medea*. There were also rough drafts of aborted poems scattered over the bedroom floor. Almost all the books were poetry.

'Are you writing poems about me?'

'I shall.'

Dinner was a bowl of olives followed by baked beans on toast. Luckily Molly was not hungry and she talked about her lunch with Colonel Bolton at The Ivy.

'Argyle smoked salmon accompanied by sloe Americano, then cauliflower masala, and then crême brulée, all with a Mersault wine. The food and drink were fabulous. But there was a price to be paid. While we were in the bar before going on to our table, Charles introduced me to Mortimer Salter, the fiction editor at *The Times Literary Supplement*. A heavy-set man with close-cropped hair and a scar on one of his cheeks, he is what you would call an ugly customer. But apparently he was one of Raven's students and he was at yesterday's funeral and Charles had invited him for a drink in The Ivy because Mortimer was so desperate to meet me. The thing is that Charles and Mortimer had been discussing putting together a *Festschrift* as a posthumous tribute to Raven, but now they think that a biography would be more appropriate and Mortimer was keen to write it. He thought that its title might be *Nevermore*. The advantage of the biography would be that it would not just cover academic matters, but also Raven's exciting and life-changing experiences in Italy. They knew that I often had had lunches with him and they hoped that he had talked to me about those years. They also hoped that I could put them in touch with Lancelyn and Bernard. They were particularly keen to get in touch with those two because, of all Raven's students, those were the ones who went on to teach English Literature at universities and presumably they had used Raven's Ignatian method in their teaching. I tried telling them that I could be of no use to them, but they were horribly insistent. As a result, I have another lunch coming up, this time with Mortimer on Wednesday at a place called *Mon Plaisir* in Covent Garden. I tried refusing, but Mortimer was hinting that he could ensure that *The Rod and the Knout* got reviewed. Or not. So on Wednesday I am stuck with a sticky lunch with Mortimer. What is more, though I did not tell Charles anything about your meeting with Bernard, Charles is convinced that it really must have been Bernard whom I saw at the funeral and he is determined to find him for me. He said that he may even resort to getting the CIA to track him down. Thanks for nothing! He thought it a bad show that Lancelyn did not turn up for the funeral. Anyway, tomorrow he flies back to Washington and doubtless he will be getting in touch with the CIA. God knows what will happen if they do discover that Bernard has had something to do with NASA. Meanwhile I am going to be stuck having lunch with Mortimer. What a mess! But first, lunch with Ferdie on Monday. I hope there will be no surprises there.'

'Why Ferdie, O Lady Who Lunches?'

'Don't look so jealous. I told you he is gay. He wants to celebrate. He has just been admitted into the Magic Circle. So he is giving me lunch at Zedel, just off Piccadilly. Marcus is so bloody jealous. It is nice to get to know other people while he is away — especially you. But I am worried that I am putting on weight.'

Since the bed was so narrow, they agreed that from now on Molly's place would be the best place for their encounters.

The following night Molly reported on her lunch with Ferdie who had been in high spirits. It was no pushover becoming a member of the Magic Circle. First, he had to find two other conjurors to recommend him. Then he had had to serve a two-year apprenticeship. Finally, there was an interview followed by a performance in front of a panel of senior conjurors. It sounded tougher than getting into Oxford. Anyway, Ferdie was elated. He had done his performance on speed, that is methedrine, and consequently his accompanying patter had been superfast. They were impressed with the patter, for patter is most important in conjuring as it can serve to misdirect the audience's attention. Then he said, 'You have the kind of looks to which it would be very easy to misdirect attention, particularly if you happened to be in a tight-fitting spangled outfit. I don't suppose that I can persuade you to serve as my conjuror's assistant on the occasional evening?'

She had said that she did not need the money, but that she would think about it. He said that he did not want to end up on stage sawing some middle-aged frump in half. Then he talked a bit about the encounter group. He was going to give it up soon. He had thought that it might serve as a kind of gay dating agency, but no luck there. Before he left the group he wanted to try out a few tricks on them and they discussed the kinds of things that might work.

Then they got into an argument about the supernatural. Ferdie claimed that his melancholy job as a conjuror was to disenchant the world, to show that the supernatural did not exist. He declared, 'A conjuror is an actor who is performing the role of a magician. On the other hand, a "magician" is a fraud pretending to be a magician. The only thing that comes close to being really supernatural is the gullibility of audiences.'

But Molly wanted to argue that the supernatural did exist and that she had seen proof of it and she described how all those years ago she and Bernard had attended a séance in St Andrews in Lancelyn's house and how, since they did not have an Ouija board, a tin of alphabet spaghetti had been produced. Marcus had brought it up to St Andrews for Janet's children who were also staying in the house for a short holiday and they tried to find to find messages from the spaghetti letters on their plates and they could not, excerpt on Lancelyn's plate where they spelt out '**WE ALL HATE YOU UNTO DEATH**'. That was spooky.

Ferdie had tapped his nose.

'Ah, the alphabet spaghetti trick! It's a good one for baffling and entertaining small groups, though it is no good on a big stage.'

'But how was it done?'

Ferdie had smiled, 'You really should have asked me last week. Then I could have told you. But now that I am a member of the Magic Circle, I have taken an oath not to reveal the secrets of any conjuring tricks.'

'But who could have done it? None of us at that séance were conjurors.'

'Ah, that I am allowed to tell you, I think. You say that it was Marcus who produced the tin of alphabet spaghetti. Was it also Marcus who afterwards got rid of the contents of the tin?'

'Yes.'

'Then obviously it has to be Marcus.'

'But why on earth would Marcus do such a thing?'

'That you will have to tell me. I don't know the man.'

Once again she had crème brûlée. Ferdie had no dessert. But when the waiter came to collect the plate, Ferdie picked up Molly's spoon, pointed it at her and watched her face as it bent before her eyes. Then he said, 'There you are. Though, you would swear that you had just watched something supernatural, I promise you that what you have just seen is merely honest deception, part of the standard conjuring repertoire.'

The waiter went to fetch the manager. Ferdie was apologetic about the spoon and suggested that it should be added to the bill, but the manager sent the waiter to bring Ferdie another spoon and asked him to do it again. Once again the spoon bent. The manager said, 'Now I have seen everything'. And, turning to the waiter, he added 'Give him twenty per cent off the bill'.

Molly concluded, 'The more I think about it, maybe Ferdie really is a magician who is pretending to be a conjuror who is acting the role of being a magician. It seems simpler to think of him in that way. But you can make your own mind up. He gave me free tickets to his next performance. Bums on seats. The tickets are for both of us, but really it is because he fancies you. I do feel at ease with Ferdie. He does not want to screw me.'

She pinched Tom on the cheek, 'You, yes.'

CHAPTER ELEVEN

Mortimer gave Molly lunch at *Mon Plaisir* in Covent Garden. Mortimer had told her his entire life story in between questioning her aggressively and, as consequence, she had forgotten what she actually ate, though she remembered that he drank whisky sours throughout the entire meal. Mortimer had begun by praising Raven to the skies. Raven was, like Chesterton, a God-intoxicated literary critic, though unfortunately, unlike Chesterton, he had left no literary legacy. After the funeral, Mortimer had conducted a not very helpful interview with Professor Tolkien. While admitting Raven's brilliance, Tolkien nevertheless told Mortimer that he felt that there was something sinister about the man and he compared him to Sauron in *Lord of the Rings*, a figure possessed by an overreaching dark ambition. Tolkien had brought the interview to an abrupt end. Molly in the restaurant wished that she could have done the same, 'He was bloody naggy, wanting to know what, if anything Raven had told me about that blasted monastery in the Apennines. In the end I started making things up and told him the sort of things that I thought that he wanted to hear. Though, of course, I said that I just could not remember where in the mountains the place was, or what its name was. I painted a picture of the noisy to and fro of war slowly giving way to the contemplation of eternity. I told him about what a great impression the abbot had made on Raven, about the hijinks that the young acolytes used to get up to, and about the rhythmical muttered prayers of the older monks. How the horrors of war and memories of the slaughter on that landing beach in Italy (whose name I also just could not remember) slowly faded as he walked round and round in the cloister and his mind started to clear. All the books in the monastery's library were in Latin, but that was no problem for Raven who had found it as easy to chat to the monks in Latin as in Italian. I told Mortimer how Raven, through conversations with learned monks, learnt how one should read the Scriptures and through reading the Scriptures, understand the world. Eventually he fell upon *The Spiritual Exercises of St Ignatius of Loyola*. And, through study of it, he came to invent a form of literary criticism that infallibly led one to God. A deep peace came upon him which hinted at the profounder peace of Paradise to come. At the end of his stay in the monastery he talked to the abbot about becoming a monk but the abbot gently took him by the hand, led him to the door and sent him out into the world where he was destined to do much good. What do I know about monasteries? Fuck all. But I enjoyed making the stuff up, for, after all, I am good at it. I am a novelist.'

She was pleased with herself. Tom was not so happy.

'That was foolish, Molly. There must be a limited number of monasteries in the Apennines. Eventually Mortimer or Charles will work their way through them and eliminate them all. And then, if Raven acquired his new name by deed poll, then presumably there will be a record of it somewhere and then they may find that under his original name he spent time in prison. And then they will want to know why you spun them such lies.'

She was annoyed, 'I had to tell him bloody something. He seemed to think that I was the guardian of some great secret about Raven.'

'You were.'

'Well anyway, after that I needed to get him off all these questions about Raven, Bernard and Lancelyn. So I asked him how come he worked at the *TLS*. He was pleased with me asking him that and he relaxed and said: '"I tell my story to myself every night before I fall asleep. My story is a strange one."'

'And it was a bit strange. He left school at fifteen without any qualifications and, because he was built for it, he found work as a nightclub bouncer. "Though when I hit them they didn't bounce back." It was easy work and he found plenty of time to read newspapers. He liked reading about riots, hostage taking, tortures in foreign parts, gangland fights and, above all, *crimes passionels*. But after a while he was sickened by what he read. It was not the subject matter that repelled him, but the awful impoverished prose that was used to describe acts of violence, love and deceit. He hated the overuse of "bloodbath", "nightmare", "traumatic", "holocaust" and "grim milestone" to describe such situations. He loathed the use of "loved ones" for family, as well as the excessive use of verbs in the passive, the unjustified application of superlatives, the ready resort to cliché and the reporters' love of platitudes. This was all becoming unbearable and so he resolved to read no more newspapers, but only proper books. The first book, picked out at random in a charity shop, was *The Duchess of Malfi*. It was followed by *The Woman in White* by Willkie Collins and the next was *Wuthering Heights*.

'After that there was no stopping him and he read voraciously for about a year before deciding that he would rather like to read English at Oxford. He chose Merton partly because T.S. Eliot had been there, but mostly because Tolkien was Professor of English at Merton. So he wrote to Tolkien, listing the books he had been reading and commenting critically on quite a few of them, before asking to be admitted to read English in that college. He got a letter back, though the reply came not from Tolkien, but from Raven, who happened to be in charge of English admissions. The letter was polite and regretful. He could not be admitted, because he had no school qualifications and there was certainly no time for him to acquire them before that year's entry exams.

'Mortimer wrote back to Raven and thanked him for clarifying the situation and then asked if it would be possible to come to Oxford to sit the examination and have it marked, simply so that he could see if he was half as good as he thought he was. Raven wrote back saying that yes, that would be possible. On the day of the examination, Mortimer had to get the milk train up to Oxford. The examination papers took most of the day. He was getting ready to walk back to the station when a college servant (they call them scouts) came up to him and told him that Mr Raven would like to see him on the following morning and that dinner and a bed could be found for him, if he was willing. The next morning another scout took him along to the room where he said that Raven would be — and so he was, together with Tolkien and three other English specialists. After the introductions, he was grilled on *Sir Gawain and the Green Knight*, *Bleak House* and the use of the subjunctive, before they got to what they seemed to be most interested in. What was life like as a bouncer?

'He went back to London. Three days later he received a letter from Raven which told him that he had been awarded a full scholarship and that further funding would be made to enable him to complete the three-year course. He did not say much about his three years there, because he knew that I was already familiar with the place and with Raven and I sort of knew what the Ignatian method was. Mortimer and Charles were a few years ahead of Bernard and Lancelyn, and, like them, they got firsts. Mortimer then went on to work for the *TLS*. It sounded most extraordinary! I had no idea that such places existed! According to Mortimer, the *TLS*, the fiercely beating heart of London's literary life, attracted hard-bitten, hard-drinking types with a taste for paratactic prose. The sort of people who cut their teeth on Hemingway and Chandler. The office was always full of cigarette smoke and, apart from the necessary telephone calls and the swearing, the place was like a morgue and editors mostly worked in silence until late afternoon.

'Mortimer said that he was in love with the adrenaline rush of editing. It was almost better than sex. An editor was a superior sort of crime-buster, whose work was to stamp out offences against English prose. The first thing he had to do when faced with a book review that had just been sent in was to look it over with a view to seeing what could be cut. It was generally a good idea to delete the first sentence. Also anything that might be used as a shout line when the paperback came out. Also passages of particularly fine writing. Those "little darlings" definitely had to be butchered. Then the piece had to be scanned for any jokes or puns. Some reviewers were cunning enough to include several jokes in what they wrote, in the hope that one might slip past the editors. Exclamation marks should be weeded out as vulgar and showy! Then there was verbal echo, which is when you repeat a word you have already used a few lines earlier. Of course, in real life people in speaking verbally echo themselves all the time. But good prose is not the same as real life. There is also something called the split infinitive. Mortimer says that writers tend to like splitting their infinitives, but for editors it is a no-no. There was also the menace of the dangling something. I have forgotten what it is that dangles and what it is supposed to do instead. The punctuation of so many contributors was like drizzle falling on a badly typed page. Mortimer found it most depressing. Commas had to be correctly placed. They had to fall with the precision of knives in a circus act, outlining the victim. Mortimer also said "Then there's speech marks. Don't get me started on that." So I didn't. More generally, the editing of punctuation was not for the faint hearted.

'Towards the end of the afternoon the whisky would come out and they would sit around on their desks, as they swapped epi-somethings from Oscar Wilde, Dorothy Parker, Montaigne and Epictetus. One was only as good as one's last epitaph, or is it one's last epigram? I get the fucking things mixed up. The editors also had some good laughs reading out passages from exceptionally pretentious reviews. Mortimer told me that he thought that, if genre fiction should be reviewed at all, sample specimens should be rounded up and placed in a crowded ghetto half-page. He had a particular dislike of historical novels. (I think that at that point he was so fired up by what he saw as the *TLS* mission that he had forgotten who he was talking to.) Picking the novelists to be reviewed was just like picking race horses at Kempton Park One went by the novelists' past finishing positions in terms of reviews and sales, also their pedigree which included where they were educated, what literary parties did they go to, and which other writers did they know.'

So that was why Tom's books of poems were not reviewed by the *TLS*! His contacts in the world of warehousing would obviously been no good to him at all. If he ever did get round to publishing the text of *The New Medea*, that would be similarly ignored. But he said nothing. Gloom had him by the throat. Molly carried on regardless, 'Then there is what they call the "bounce factor" when an author, who has not published for a long time, suddenly produces another novel. This could be because he has been working on the great masterpiece for a very long time. On the other hand, he or she could just be burnt out and therefore the belated product would be no good at all. Literary gossip might help there. The bounce factor is not to be confused with the "dead cat bounce", which is when a particular author is thought to be dead, but then he or she went on and produced another novel. Barbara Pym might be a case in point. Inevitably there were always snap decisions to be made before the presses rolled. Often there was a standoff about what should be the lead fiction review. Should Iris Murdoch take precedence over C.P. Snow? Sometimes this sort of thing was decided by the toss of a coin, but on one occasion it was decided by a wrestling match with three falls the clincher. The *TLS* reviewers are handpicked for aggression and necessarily protected by the assassin's cloak of anonymity.'

Perhaps it was just as well that his poems had not been reviewed.

'So that was the *TLS* and I thought dinner was over and that Mortimer had finished, but then he threw a bit of a bloody zinger at me. He had been checking the *TLS* archive for who wrote the killer review of Bernard's book. (By the way, he found the review hilarious.) After that brutal send-up of academic pretension, its victim might well want to go into hiding and change his name. Mortimer found out that it was Bernard's best friend, Lancelyn, who wrote that review of Bernard's book about ghost stories. Did I know that? What was going on there? What had happened between Bernard and Lancelyn? I could deny almost all knowledge of this since, though Raven did tell me that Lancelyn had written that review, I never got around to asking Lancelyn why he had done such a shocking thing. So there it was. I had anticipated that this was going to be a bloody awkward lunch, and so it was, in fact even worse than I had anticipated, and now Mortimer is threatening me with another lunch date. Of course, he wants to bed me. He must see that as coming with the lunches. But I also get the sense that he and Charles imagine themselves as some kind of game hunters and that they are planning to use me as a sort of tethered goat to lure Lancelyn and Bernard out of their lairs. It was as if they were going to assign me a subsidiary part in someone else's story. I don't want that.'

Looking back on what Molly had said, Tom thought that personally he might go further. Not only did he not want to be part of Charles and Mortimer's story, whatever that might be, he did not want to be part of Molly's story either, and he did not even want to be part of his own story. In his case, there was not much of a story to call his own. He also could not believe that it could be true that working at the *TLS* really was quite that tough. Mortimer was just talking it up to make himself look big. And Tom was getting fed up with clever people. They were so competitive, such as those *TLS* types trading epitaphs. Their monstrous brains seethed with ideas like so many lumps of meat which were seen to heave because they were infested by so many maggots, while their swift tongues were like the tails of scorpions.

CHAPTER TWELVE

Ferdie was billed to perform in a small theatre a little way off Upper Regent Street. Posters outside the theatre proclaimed 'The great Zamboni presents the mysterious wonder show of the universe'. Playing cards, trumpets and disembodied heads floated in the poster's background and horned and winged little demons were shown scuttling about the master magician as they worked to assist him in his tricks. Though Ferdie was shown wearing conventional evening dress, his protruding shocks of hair were now concealed by a turban.

The show consisted of fairly conventional tricks, but there were so many of them! Ferdie delivered his tricks at such speed, that it was difficult to take it all in, as one trick segued into another. He seemed to be trying to cram as many things as possible into an hour and a half. Moreover, the accompanying patter was delivered at a velocity that made it difficult to concentrate on both it and the tricks. Perhaps his gabble was a way of misdirecting the attention? A nervous looking girl brought him a top hat from which he produced a live rabbit, a pigeon, a balloon, and a birthday cake with all its candles alight. He extended his arms towards a chair on the edge of the stage and he seemed to force it to levitate. The nervy girl passed a hoop round the chair to show that no wires were involved. He ran among the stalls and produced playing cards, coins and, on one occasion, a mouse from the clothes, handbags or ears of members of the audience. And so on. The girl was looking exhausted, but Ferdie seemed desolate when the manager signalled that his time was definitely up. The applause was as much for the energy as for the magic.

Afterwards Tom and Molly visited him in his dressing room.

Ferdie made them welcome, 'Thank you for coming — as the actress said to the bishop.'

With his turban now off, his spikey hair once again stood out on either side of his head. Molly complimented him on his performance and its velocity. He interrupted before she could quite finish, 'Speed is of the essence — by which I mean methedrine. It's great for the patter, as well as for the sex, and it keeps me slim. Though it does feel like riding a tiger — terrific when you are on his back — but, when you have to come down off him, it will be dangerous. The tiger will keep prowling around and the safest thing to do often seems to be to jump once more onto his back. I have always loved tigers. Happily I have this beast under control. I tell you, if you want some real magic, here it is in this box.'

This was all in a gabble. And he opened the box which contained the little glass ampoules of methedrine.

Molly and Tom gazed at the ampoules, not knowing what to say. Finally, Molly changed the subject, 'Zamboni is a great stage name.'

'Thank you. I felt that Ferdinand Harris would not have served me so well. As for "Zamboni", last year a friend took me to the ice rink at Queensway and, during an interval, while the rink was cleared of ice skaters, a majestic great machine came out and was slowly driven round to collect all the ice shavings and spread a thin layer of water on top of the ice. Zamboni is an ice resurfacer. I took careful note of the name, thinking that I might have a use for it. But the Zamboni machine is slow and methodical, whereas I am fast, for speed helps me race through life and take in everything and see all the connections. Yet, for me, speed is not enough. This evening I was just performing a traditional repertoire, the sorts of tricks that can be seen on seaside piers and even at children's parties. Give me time and the Great Zamboni will rise above all that.'

And now he reached into the pocket of his dinner jacket and produced some tissue paper which he unfolded to reveal some sugar cubes.

'LSD. A very different drug. It takes me into a world of carnival bright colours wherein I behold an endless and plotless parade of marvels. So many brilliantly illuminated doors of perception are opened to me and, looking through, I glimpse tricks that have rarely been performed or, in some cases never. On one recent trip a door opened on the ritual of the transposed heads. I later looked it up in the library of the Magic Circle. The feat has only once been attempted in Germany some decades back and I am not sure that it was successful. Before I die I shall demonstrate the business of the transposed heads, for it is a beautiful and mysterious thing to behold. The thing is that the trick is that there is no trick. The heads are really transposed.'

Molly protested, 'But that would be magic!'

'Yes.'

Now Molly was even more indignant, 'But when we were in the Zedel you assured me that there was no such thing as the supernatural!'

'When we were at the restaurant I was not high on any drug, but I say different things when I am on drugs and what I say will depend on what drug I am on. I am a different person on LSD and different again when I have taken opium. This evening I have yet to come down from the methedrine and one of the things about methedrine is that it makes one want to reach out and confide in people. It makes me want to embrace… you… both… so now, Molly, I can tell you that magic is real. A hidden magic infuses the normal and the natural. It merely uses misdirection of attention in order to stay hidden…'

Now Tom, sensing that at last he had found a man who shared his poetic vision broke in, 'I know what you are talking about. I have felt this too. Magical folk are hidden, but sometimes I have sensed their presence and I have thought that I have seen them hidden in the little whirlwinds of leaves that rise up off the pavements. I think dogs can see them too and they try to chase them away. Also the find-the-lady men I have watched in various parts of London. They are trickster fairies pretending to be ordinary conmen.'

Ferdie tapped his nose.

'Ah yes. I call them the three-card-Monte operators. Some of them are indeed fairies. But you know, these days a lot of them are ordinary mortals. There was a time when all the practitioners of the three-card Monte were fairies and they could make the queen of hearts appear wherever they wished just by wishing on it. Sadly, real magic has been declining in this country for centuries and the 1960s was the last chance for the fairies and now they are being replaced by conmen, just as magicians give way to conjurors. Boat by boat the fairies have been crossing the Atlantic. The USA is now the last bastion of magic.'

Molly stood listening with her mouth open. She was appalled.

Ferdie looked at her apologetically.

'Tomorrow I will be a straight person again and then I will be able to reassure you that there is no such thing as real magic. There are only such trumpery things as sleight-of-hand, cunningly devised contraptions and misdirected attention. Ferdie is several people. So it is, if Ferdie has to make a major decision, they take it first while Ferdie is high on one drug or another, but then then check that decision when Ferdie has come down from the drug. If the two verdicts do not agree, then another drug is taken, usually the subtle and wise old opium, in order to come to a majority decision. Would you like to try some opium?'

Molly shook her head emphatically, 'Thank you so much, Ferdie, but I think we have to be going. You will be very careful with all these drugs, won't you?'

He smiled sadly.

'My feeling is that I do not have time to be careful. I shall burn up, yes, but when my body is all burnt out I shall take on another. At least, that is what I think this evening. Tomorrow I may tell you another story.'

Once they were out of the theatre, Molly said to Tom, 'I didn't like that one little bit. We were stuck having a conversation not with Ferdie, but with some wretched fluid that comes in a little bottle.'

Later yet, when they were both in bed, Molly wanted to know if Tom had read her novel yet and what did he think of it. The gun was once again pressed against his head.

Just then the phone rang. Saved by the bell.

'That will be sodding Mortimer.'

But when she came into the bedroom, 'That was Marcus. He's flying back tomorrow.'

So no more nights with Molly and her gun. Was he about to step off the Carousel of Adventure? Not quite.

CHAPTER THIRTEEN

Two evenings later, as he was leaving the warehouse, Tom's way was blocked by a tall, heavily built man with a scar on his cheek. Evidently the fiction editor of *The Times Literary Supplement*.

'You are Thomas the Rhymer?'

'My name is Tom Byrne.'

'Just so. I thought we might take a little walk. I gather that you think of yourself as a poet. So, Mr Poet, what rhymes with Mortimer?

'I don't think anything rhymes with Mortimer.'

'My name is Mortimer Salter by the way. Carnivore rhymes with Mortimer. So do forefinger, harbinger and Terpsichore. Not much of a rhymer are you?'

Though Tom did not think that those were good rhymes and, anyway, one should not pronounce the name of the muse of dance the way that Mortimer did, it seemed wiser to keep quiet on these matters.

Mortimer continued, 'Still, good luck with the poetry and that, of course, is not why I am here. The thing is I have been told by someone who was told by you that you were working as Molly Ransom's bodyguard and I was wondering how come and also whether you only served her as her bodyguard.'

'Wonder away. I don't think that is any business of yours.'

'Such a lollapalooza of a beautiful woman should not belong to just one man, but I don't think you quite realise what you are getting into with her… that dame is both screwy and deadly. What I do know is that it's certain that she drove Lancelyn Delderfield insane and it's also possible that she has murdered Bernard. I would value your take on all of this. So perhaps I might accompany you on your way back to your flat and we may talk as we go. Carcanet gave me your address, by the way.'

Tom said nothing.

Mortimer was silent for a while as they walked, but then resumed the interrogation, 'May I ask how you and Molly met?'

'We met at an encounter group and were assigned each other as co-counsellors.'

What the fuck is an encounter group? What is co-counselling?'

Tom tried to explain. To which Mortimer responded, 'The world is full of trendy wonders and mysteries and you have just introduced me to a new one.'

By now they were at Tom's front door. He paused and Mortimer said, 'Now I think you should invite me in and perhaps offer me a tot or two of whisky.'

Though Mortimer's voice was perfectly pleasant, some-how there was a feeling of definite menace about his proposal. He was not to be denied. Mortimer wanted some lemon with his whisky. Once he was contentedly settled, he resumed his investigation.

'As I am sure that you know, Molly and I had lunch a few days ago and she was able to provide me with colourful details about Raven's time in an Italian monastery.' He paused. 'It was, of course, a pack of lies. I know fiction when I come across it. It is my job. Bad prose always betrays itself, like an incompetent thief whose fingerprints are all over the scene of the crime. So now I want to know from you, what is she hiding? Why did she need a bodyguard? What was her connection with Raven, Bernard and Lancelyn in Oxford? Then what went on in St Andrews all those years ago? Where is Bernard now? Where is Lancelyn? I should warn you that I already know the answers to some of those questions, so I will soon know if you tell me any lies. I may have been born stupid, but I'm getting cleverer year by year. Also, don't try and pull a gun on me. The last person who did so is regretting it. More whisky please.'

Mortimer was so intimidating. Tom inconsequentially wondered if he should put Mortimer in *The New Medea* as the tyrant of Colchis. And then perhaps Mortimer might have ideas about what rhymed with Colchis.

So then Tom explained how Molly had taken him on as a bodyguard because she was scared of a lecturer on Scottish Literature who was stalking her and who had recently acquired a gun. He then told Mortimer about accompanying Molly to the funeral and how he had subsequently encountered Bernard by chance and he went on to relate as much as he could remember of Bernard's story about the Bradbury Institute. Why not? After all, he owed Bernard nothing. If anything, Bernard owed him a pint. As an afterthought, Tom gave an account of a conversation with an academic called Quentin and what Quentin had told him about Lancelyn's uncertain whereabouts.

Mortimer nodded thoughtfully.

'It was Quentin who gave me your name and then, as I say, Carcanet gave me your address. Now, have you ever visited St Andrews?'

Tom shook his head.

'I hadn't either until last week, but it was becoming clear to me that things that had happened in that place some ten years back were the key to the disappearances of Bernard and Lancelyn. So I went to St Andrews and I did not like what I found there. It's a strange story, "as strange as a dreamer's mad imaginings". The town was enveloped in a wintery mist which they call the haar and its icy fingers clawed at my heart. The street lights were surrounded by rainbow haloes. The place was like an open-air funeral parlour. There was hardly anyone in the streets and the few living people I did encounter looked as if they might be better off dead. I walked about a bit to get my bearings. There is a ruined cathedral with a tower which I was told was a great favourite among would-be suicides. Eventually I located the English Department and asked if I could have a quick meeting with its head. There was a longish wait before Professor Barkworth could see me. Fortunately I had Walter Pater's *The Renaissance: Studies in Art and Poetry* with me. Do you know it?

Tom shook his head.

'You should. The man who wrote "To burn always with this hard, gem-like flame, to maintain this ecstasy, is success in life", deserves the reverence of every kind of artist, poets included. We all must die, but Pater's prose suggests that there

is a definite beauty in that very fact. Such a musical stylist…
I digress. My meeting with Professor Barkworth was brief.
He had indeed heard that there was some sort of scandal
concerning Lancelyn's breakdown, but it was before his time.
Perhaps those who were members of the department in the
sixties could shed more light on the matter. He suggested that
I speak to Henry Carleton or Jaimie Hay. I found Carleton in
his office in the department. The old guy looked like another
of those who might be better off dead. He was not keen on
looking back on what was past, but he talked briefly about
how, for a few days after Lancelyn was starting to show signs
of emotional strain, he had taken over his special subject and
how he had then called on his house in Hepburn Gardens to
consult him about some points arising from teaching and how
he had inadvertently walked in on some kind of orgy in which
Lancelyn, Jaimie and a floozy brought up to St Andrews from
England were involved. Lancelyn's scholarly mansion had
been turned into a cat house. Henry, who had all the vitality of
a dried fish, was not hot to join in and he had just turned tail
and fled. So that was it, I thought, but then he mentioned that
there was a friend of Lancelyn called Quentin in the History
Department and that it was this man who had taken the can of
paraffin from Lancelyn, before summoning medical help to get
Lancelyn out of the staff common room and into an ambulance
that would take him to a mental hospital in Dundee.

'It sounded like I really needed to get to this Jaimie, but
he was not in the department that day. So I thought that I might
get a little more background from this Quentin guy, whom I
did find in his department. He looked like a cross between
an oriental sage and a hen's egg. He was happy to talk about

how he had got his good friend Lancelyn carted off to the loony bin after he seemed to be about to start a new career as a pyromaniac. I wanted to know which loony bin. Maybe I could visit or perhaps rescue him from it. But Quentin told me that Lancelyn had been out for years and he was sailing his big yacht on one of the world's oceans, probably the South Seas, and that Jaimie's former mistress, a dumb blonde called, Sylvie something, was his shipboard companion. I thought that, since this Sylvie was travelling the world in luxury with a handsome and clever man, then, as blondes go, she was not so dumb. However, I wanted Quentin to carry on talking, so I kept this thought to myself.

Quentin also mentioned that Sylvie had once been Jaimie Hay's mistress. So it was definitely him I needed to see and I said so to Quentin. However, he warned me that this Jaimie character seemed to be turning into a hoplophiliac. What the hell was that? It turned out to be some kind of freak who got sexual arousal from guns.'

Tom wondered if hoplophilia could be contagious. Certainly he and Molly had been getting a lot of sexual pleasure from her gun.

Mortimer continued, 'Jaimie had acquired a pistol which he even occasionally brandished during his lectures and the head of the department was too scared to do anything about it. The other thing Quentin was able to tell me about was that weirdo séance in Lancelyn's house, where the spaghetti letters of doom threatened Lancelyn with death. It was during this séance that Quentin was able to determine that something sexual was going on between Molly and Lancelyn, since he spotted that she had unbuttoned his flies and she sure as hell wasn't fumbling for ectoplasm.

'I thought that I ought to see the house which had served as a kind of theatre for the séance, then the orgy and finally the descent of Lancelyn into madness. It was only a step away. Everything is only a step away in St Andrews and Quentin offered to take me there. After all that had happened in that great mansion in Hepburn Gardens, the place was reputed to be spooked and it was impossible to sell it. So the interior had been divided up and rented out as student flats and, yeah, the students looked pretty spooked to me. One of them showed me the room where the séance took place. I tried to catch a sinister aura, but it was just sad. Just a messy student flat.

'So that was the haunted cathouse. It was now time to pay Jaimie Hay a visit. His cottage, a ramshackle affair that had taken quite a battering from the elements, was on the harbour waterfront. I knocked and the door was opened promptly by a man who looked like the sort of cherub who took lots of healthy outdoor exercise. I introduced myself as a friend of Molly Ransom and gave my name and he, all smiles, confirmed that he was Jaimie and invited me in. A young woman was lying on the sofa, but Jaimie ordered Saffron up and told her to go out and take a walk for an hour or two. Then he turned to me smiling.

"Dear Molly! How is she?"

"I had lunch with her a few days ago and she was in good spirits."

"That is good to hear. And what does she do these days?"

"She works at Sotheby's and…"

At this point Tom interrupted, 'Jaimie Hay has a pretty good idea how she is and he already knew that she works for

Sotheby's. He is the Scottish lecturer who has been stalking her.'

'So I had surmised,' said Mortimer calmly. 'Then he wanted to know if I worked for Sotheby's too and I told him that, no, I worked for *The Times Literary Supplement*. (I could see that he was impressed by that.) Then I said that I was trying to find out more about a former contributor, one Lancelyn Delderfield.

'Then Jaimie went on a long dithyramb about what a dear friend Lancelyn had been. He was so fond of him that he could even say he loved the man, him and Molly together. That said, though he loved the man, he could see that Lancelyn was very reserved and somewhat arrogant, so proud of his weird library and his wealth. Jamie and Molly tried to show him what fun sex could and should be — often literally, as they demonstrated various sexual positions in front of him. They were young and it was the sixties and the rest of the town was so stuffy. Jaimie and Molly also showed him how receiving pain could be sexually pleasurable. At the same time they had wanted to teach him humility and they had instructed him in how to take a practical interest in such household things as cleaning, tidying up and making beds. It was like one long house party, all with the aim of making him a better, more rounded person. Jaimie said that Lancelyn was ridiculously proud not only of having been at Oxford, but also of having been a favoured student of an old pervert called Raven. At which point I thought that I should call time on the distasteful dithyramb. I let him know that I had also been at Oxford and that I too had been a favoured student of Raven's. "Ah." He evidently found some difficulty in believing this.

'But now he started to gabble. He and "darling" Lancelyn had been at a meeting with the former professor, a man called Wormsley, when the professor revealed that he had known Raven in his previous incarnation. Apparently Edward Burbottle was a school chaplain who was arrested and convicted as a paedophile. He spent most of the war years in prison and it was there that he invented the Ignatian technique and reinvented himself as Raven by changing his name by deed poll. When Jaimie saw that it looked as though I was about to thump him one, he hastily added that this was all checkable. Burbottle's conviction was reported in the papers and doubtless there was also some record of his changing his name by deed poll. Moreover Molly was present when Lancelyn later confronted Raven with all this. Raven could not deny it. He was even rather proud of the way he had reconstructed himself.'

Now Mortimer looked to Tom, 'Did you know anything about this?'

'Yes. Molly told me on the train when we were on the way to Raven's funeral.'

'That woman… layer upon layer upon layer of lies and reticence and, as it turns out, those lies and evasions have been mostly about a man who was himself a master of deceit. I have been reduced to the role of a scavenger who picks through those layers of falsehood. If only the real world could be strictly nonfiction… so Jaimie had given me a lot to think about. It was clear that a biography of Raven would be a very bad idea and I ought to go away and decide what to do next. I rose to leave. But Jaimie begged me to sit while he fetched some things from the other room. He came back with a proof copy of *The Problem of Evil in the Scottish Novel* and a gun. The book was due to be published in a couple of months' time. He handed the proof to me and wanted my assurance that it would be reviewed in the *TLS*. I said that this was not within my remit, as I was the fiction editor. But he said he was sure that I could fix it for the book to be reviewed. I said that I hoped it would be and our chat had been most interesting and now I had to be going, but he motioned me to stay sitting and said that it was evident that I had not understood the significance of his book.

'He would give me an idea of its importance by giving me just a hint of one chapter. This was the chapter on Stevenson's *Treasure Island*. As a boy Jaimie had loved adventure stories, especially that one, and he knew the book by heart. Indeed he quoted whole paragraphs to me. Apart from the mother of Jim Hawkins, there are no women in *Treasure Island*. That is how all adventures should be. Women in novels just cloud men's brains and slow down the action. More important, Jaimie had worshipped the novel's hero and hoped to model himself on him when he grew up. Silver was a gentleman of fortune, who had had many adventures. He was always smiling, resolute and courageous. Also clever. And despite the missing leg, he was without self-pity and he was full of vitality. He was ruthless when necessary, genial when not. The two-hundred-year-old parrot called Captain Flint, who sat on Silver's shoulder was the final flamboyant touch and a kind of custodian of a heroic piratical past. Jaimie carried his devotion to Silver so far that as a boy he wished that he might have one of his legs amputated and replaced by a wooden one.

'Jaimie continued that it was great shock to him when he

finally arrived at Edinburgh University and started to read the so-called critical literature on the book. The so-called critics took it for granted that a dull and colourless boy called Jim Hawkins was the hero of the story (backed up by two gents called Livesey and Trelawney). That was the ridiculous orthodoxy and what a greedy trio they make! What right did those three have over the treasure? It was men like Pew and Bones and Silver who had fought and fought hard for it. Moreover, the real story was not what the naïve reader saw on the printed page. The real story had already happened. Flint dead, Pew blinded, Silver losing his leg, treasure buried, Gunn marooned. Everybody who mattered was in the grip of the past.

'Simple-minded readers, and it had to be admitted most of its readers were either children or academic critics, simple-minded readers were misled by the fact that the story is all told from the viewpoint of Jim Hawkins. Simple-minded readers tend unthinkingly to identify with the character who is providing the narrative viewpoint in the story — even to the point that they are likely to find themselves identifying with the murderers in certain fictions of Poe and Dostoevsky. So it is that the naïve will tend to back Hawkins in this adventure, even though that adventure has already happened, very likely before the boy was born.

'At this point,' Mortimer said, 'I interrupted and asked what had all this to do with the problem of evil. Also I did not take kindly to being given a lecture on a children's book. He gave me a peculiar smile and replied that the trouble with evil was that it could never be unmixed. It was like coffee and cream. One poured the coffee and then added the cream and stirred it in. But one could never unstir the cream in a coffee. Was I following him? I was not and, though it was evident that he was only just getting started on the beauty of evil, I had had enough of his cracker-barrel literary criticism. I told him that I had found this all most interesting, but now I had to go and I stood up.

But Jaimie picked up the gun on the table, pointed it at me and said, "If a review of *Problem of Evil in the Scottish Novel* is not published in the *TLS* in the next couple of months, I will come after you with this gun." (It was a .46 by the way.) In retrospect, it was possible that his making the threat might have been a joke, but this was not the first time I had been held at gunpoint and I could not let him have the benefit of the doubt. I fell to the floor in a seeming faint. When I opened my eyes and fluttered my eyelashes, I saw that Jaimie was leaning over me and looking concerned. I head-butted him and his head shot up and his nose started to bleed. Then I punched him in the throat. Then I rolled out of the way of his dripping blood, stood up and kicked the gun away. Then I pulled out his right arm from under him and stamped on his wrist. Then I stamped on it again to make sure it was properly broken. Then I pocketed the gun. Nobody messes with the fiction editor of *The Times Literary Supplement*.'

Mortimer was looking hard at Tom as he said this, but continued, "Jaimie Hay, you have the face of a bonny wee lassie but, if we ever meet again I will spoil your face by putting your mouth where an ear is."

Then Mortimer looked sadly at his empty glass and the empty bottle.

'Why have I been telling you all this? Because my trip

to St Andrews has been instructive. Above all, I learnt how dangerous Molly is. Did you notice that *fleur-de-lis* tattoo on her arm?'

'What about it?'

'When she was a schoolgirl she read *The Three Musketeers* by Alexandre Dumas and ever since she has wished that she could live in an age when dashing heroes and heroines served Kings, Dukes and Cardinals, rather than the common good. More specifically she identifies herself with the novel's Milady de Winter. I would even go so far as to say that she regards herself as a reincarnation of this fictional character.'

'Who is the lady in question?'

'Milady de Winter is a beautiful and ruthless spy in the service of Cardinal Richelieu. As a young nun she seduced a priest and together they ran off with the takings from the church. After being caught and imprisoned, she seduced the gaoler's son and so escaped. But a little later an executioner caught up with her and branded her with the *fleur-de-lis* to mark her as a common criminal. The Musketeer Athos married her, but when he discovered the *fleur-de-lis*, he had her hanged from a tree, but, unknown to Athos, she survived this hanging and would go on to murder the English nobleman whom she had subsequently married. She made several attempts to murder D'Artagnan, engineered the murder of the Duke of Buckingham, and succeeded in murdering D'Artagnan's mistress. Finally the Musketeers tracked her down and oversaw her beheading. But the tattoo which Athos, D'Artagnan and the general readership of the novel identify as an incriminating badge of shame has been taken by Molly to be a badge of honour. She is a foe to men and I am here to advise you to have nothing to do with her.'

'I had already decided that.'

Mortimer nodded approvingly.

'You are not part of all this. At least you do not have to be. Thank you for your hospitality. One last thing. Did Bernard say where he was going next?'

'There was nothing definite. But you might try the Society for Psychical Research.'

'I will and thank you again for your time and the whisky. Oh, yet another one last thing. Have you read Molly's novel?

'I found it so colourful that in the end I took to skimming it.'

Mortimer nodded approvingly, 'Her book is so bad that it will have a wide appeal, since stupid people who speak bad prose like to read stupid stories written in bad prose and such paltry fictions confirm their sense of self-worth.'

With Mortimer gone, Tom was at last free to laugh. He just could not imagine Mortimer fluttering his eyelashes.

CHAPTER FOURTEEN

So that was that, Tom thought. He would have to leave Marcus and Mortimer and maybe Jaimie and God knows who else to fight over Molly. Perhaps he should have warned Mortimer about Marcus' return and his possessive character and proneness to violence, as well as the fact that Molly had acquired a gun. But a few days later the phone rang. It was Molly.

'Tom I need your help. I need your help badly.'

'Molly, my bodyguarding days are over. Surely Marcus can pay for your protection?'

'It's not that. You sound so surly, darling Tom. The thing is, Lancelyn has turned up. He sent me a letter, care of my publisher. He wants to meet me.'

'Well, won't that be nice? The main reason you went to that funeral was that you hoped that you would see Lancelyn again so that you could apologise and make it up with him.'

'I know. I know. Stop making this so hard for me. The thing is that I have now got cold feet. What Jaimie and I did to him is probably unforgiveable. I wouldn't be surprised if Lancelyn tied me up in a sack and threw me into the sea. During that awful, wonderful week in St Andrews Jaimie taught me how pleasurable evil can be and he awakened me to the sense of my sexual power. At the same time, I took pleasure in submitting to Jaimie. The pleasure was heightened when this was done in front of Lancelyn. The look of meek suffering in his eyes just made me want to laugh. There were so many vile and dirty things to explore. But now I wish that confession really was good for the soul.'

'OK. So ignore the letter.'

'No, I want absolution, some form of forgiveness. I need to know that he is not going to seek me out and kill me. Also has he fully regained his sanity? I want you to go for me, talk to him and, if you can, obtain my absolution. I will pay you.'

'That is insulting. I am not interested in your money.'

'Sorry… but it might be expensive to get to Cowes.'

'Cowes! That is on the Isle of Wight isn't it? I am not going all the way to Cowes to talk apologetically to a complete stranger. Not for any amount of money.'

'Dear Tom. You must. I am pretty sure that I have spotted Jaimie and he has resumed his bloody stalking. I don't want him following me down to Cowes and trying to resume things with Lancelyn and me. But he doesn't know anything about you. Not money then, but something better. On one of those nights when you are on warehouse duty, I will tell Marcus that I have gone to spend the night with an aged aunt. Then I will come to the warehouse and you could show me how it works and teach me about its beauty, and I would bring along rugs and cushions and, of course, the gun. You can have first turn with the gun. It will be new and sort of exciting, making love in your warehouse.'

'Cowes it is.'

'Bless you Tom. He will be expecting me at the Royal London Yacht Club in Cowes Sunday after next.'

The Cowes clubhouse was a large Regency building. Tom gave his name at reception and said that he had been sent by Molly Ransom to carry a message to Lawrence Delderfield. A few minutes later a puzzled looking man came down the stairs. He was handsome in a tanned, weather-beaten sort of way and was wearing a blazer and scarf. This must be Lancelyn. Uncertainly he advanced on Tom.

'You must be Mr Byrne. Have we met before? My memory is not what it once was.'

Tom shook his head.

'Well then. What has brought you here and what is Miss Ransom's message?

'It is a long story.'

'I see. In that case you had better follow me and you can tell me whatever the message is over a few drinks.'

Tom followed Lancelyn to the bar of the clubroom. There he was introduced to Sylvie, the dumb or not so dumb blonde, who was seated on a sofa. Beside her, an open copy of *Mr Majestyk* was face down on the sofa.

Tom took a seat opposite to Lancelyn and Sylvie and then Lancelyn ordered gin and tonics all round.

'Have you read Elmore Leonard? Frightfully good... well then, what is your business?'

'It is hard to know where to begin... I am a friend of Molly's. She has sent me here to apologise and to seek your forgiveness for what happened in St Andrews.'

Sylvie glared at Tom. Lancelyn merely looked anxious.

'You are going to have to explain and start wherever

you think the beginning is. My memory is not what it once was. After my breakdown I was given ECT, electro-shock therapy that is. It was, I think, pretty horrible, like an induced epileptic fit, though I hardly remember anything of it or what happened in the days immediately before my breakdown. Memory loss is a common side effect of the treatment. It is called "retrograde amnesia". I had thought that seeing Molly again might bring back memories. Also I think I have got what is called "cognitive impairment". I am not as clever as I once was, though I don't mind this, as it makes me more like normal people. I find I like normality very much. The last thing I remember properly before the end of my shock treatment and transfer to a sanatorium in the south of England, is my being a terribly clever person who was travelling up to St Andrews with Molly. We were on a train from Edinburgh to St Andrews and Molly, sitting beside me, had fallen asleep. So she was missing the beautiful deserted beaches of Burntisland and Kinghorn and the angry sea that glittered in the gathering dark. I was thinking how voluptuously beautiful she was. But perhaps the angriness of the sea was an omen... Sylvie refuses to talk about what happened thereafter. She is not a great talker...'

'Talking is not what I am good at,' said Sylvie who stuck out her tongue at Lancelyn before adding, 'I am not going to stay to hear what I fear is coming. I am going for a walk.'

Once she was gone, Lancelyn said, 'Fire away.'

'Why not just forgive Molly for however she may have wronged you without knowing the details? It is not a pleasant story. I really don't think you want to hear what I can tell you and, besides, I was not a witness to what went on in Hepburn

Gardens that terrible week. I have just picked up scraps from what Mortimer, Quentin and Jaimie have said. I don't know the whole story and it is possible I may have misunderstood some of it. Are you certain you want to hear it?'

'Quentin and I write to each other occasionally… and I do remember Jaimie. Mortimer, I don't know. Jaimie was nuts on Scottish Literature. My past is behind me and the truth cannot harm me. I would like to hear the story, for I am a bit like Winnie the Pooh. I like to hear stories about myself. '

'This is not going to be a Winnie the Pooh story.'

And then Tom told Lancelyn all that he had been able to piece together of that final week in St Andrews: Jaimie's installation in Lancelyn's house and his seduction of Molly, the orgy à *trois* and the sadistic humiliation of Lancelyn which led to his purchasing a can of paraffin with the intention perhaps of burning the house down. When Tom had finished, Lancelyn smiled gently and said, 'Thank you. Somehow that all sounds rather fun. I just wish I could remember it. I suppose I must always have had a masochistic streak. I sometimes think I would like to return to Scotland, the site of lost memory, lost youth and of lost love. It was so beautiful, though I fear that there would be nothing there for me now. We have no home except our yacht and so I have become a gypsy millionaire. I am getting peckish. When Sylvie gets back, we must all have lunch together. I hope they will still be serving. Is there anything else?'

Tom started to tell him about what Quentin had observed at the séance, as well as Ferdie's insistence that the business with the spaghetti letters was a well-established conjuring trick, but Lancelyn put up his hand, 'No, I do remember that.

But your friend is quite wrong about the way the spaghetti letters fell out being a conjuring trick. By now I have seen enough of the world to know that there is such a thing as the supernatural. I have been privileged to observe its workings not once, but twice. Shall I tell you of my second encounter with the supernatural? My story is a strange one.

'Together with Sylvie and a small crew, I have been sailing the world. We started off exploring the Caribbean, before moving on to the Indian Ocean and then the South Seas. There we ended up docking in the bottle-shaped harbour of Apia, the capital of Samoa. The place was a bit of a dump. Entering the harbour, we looked across to rusting wrecks, derelict warehouses, dingy bars and low-level houses with wood smoke rising from their chimneys. The dense tropical vegetation tumbled down the hills and threatened to engulf the outlying shanties. Later I learned that we had chosen to make landfall at what was known as 'the Hell of the Pacific'.

'Nevertheless Sylvie and I were desperate to get our land legs back. The boat needed some careening. Also I had run out of reading matter and I was hoping to buy some more thrillers or whodunnits. I did find a few. We took walks along the beaches beyond the harbour. There were no tourists on the beaches. We watched beachcombers foraging among the jetsam and seashore sorcerers holding consultations on the sand. We collected shells and sat listening to the sound of the waves breaking far out over coral reefs. Away from the ramshackle harbour settlement, the luxuriant greens of the forest, the explosions of hibiscus and frangipani blossoms and the glitter of the sea under a blazing blue sky was just too much technicolour and I found myself wishing for the softer tones of the Scottish landscape.

'After a couple of days, we were bored and on the third day I decided that we should set out to the nearby village of Vailima where Robert Louis Stevenson had lived and died and make the ascent to his tomb which was at the top of Mount Vaea, more for the exercise than for any other reason. Though I used to be a real expert on the classics of English Literature — and Scottish Literature even — I put all that behind me after my breakdown and I no longer had any special interest in difficult writers, including Stevenson. So his tomb was an arbitrary goal. The Sun was barely up when we started our walk and we soon reached the foot of the thickly forested mountain. By the time we began our ascent the heat was building up and we were glad to enter the tropical gloom of the woods. As we climbed, I gave Sylvie a mini-lecture based on what I could remember of Stevenson's final years in the South Seas and the books he wrote during that time, *The Ebb Tide*, *Catriona* and *Island Nights Entertainments*, and how he was working on what might have been the finest of all his novels, *Weir of Hermiston*, when in 1894 he was suddenly felled by a stroke.

'As we neared the peak, it seemed that we were in for a disappointment. Not that we were all that disappointed. The tomb was completely surrounded by mounds of reddish earth and wickerwork rattan screens on which were affixed signs announcing that repair and restoration work was going on and warning that it was dangerous to approach the tomb. I was a bit puzzled by this as I had seen photos of the tomb and it looked to be a most solid construction of concrete slabs. How could these slabs require restoration work and what was all the digging for? We sat down a little way from it. After a few minutes three men emerged from behind one of the screens. One of them came over and introduced himself as Keola and asked if he could sit with us and rest. It is like that in bars, parks and beaches across the world. Men like to sit close to Sylvie. Keola was a fleshy man who was wearing a skirt-like garment, which I believe is called a *lavalava*, but who was otherwise barechested and sweating heavily. He planted himself close to Sylvie and smiled ingratiatingly.

'You are tourists?'

'I suppose so. We have been travelling the world for years. What on earth is going on here?'

'We are repairing the grave of this Stevenson. This Stevenson was a great man. You know about this Stevenson?'

I nodded. At which point he started to quiz me about Stevenson, his life and his writings in some detail. I felt as if I was back in time, once again a university lecturer and giving a tutorial on *Dr Jekyll and Mr Hyde*, *Treasure Island* and *The Master of Ballantrae*.

He was impressed. Finally he said, 'So you really know his stories. You know also that he was a rich man. Very rich. Here at Vailima he purchased 314 acres and he built some grand buildings on his land. He was known as *tusitala* which means the teller of stories. Now one does not get rich telling stories. Rangi and I tell stories. Many of my friends tell stories. We are not rich. Even people on this island who are hired to write things down for big companies do not become rich. I think that it is not true that telling stories made this Stevenson rich. We know that because he wrote something about the source of his money and it has been translated into Samoan. The missionaries had it printed to warn us islanders of the dangers of magic. But the danger of magic is little compared to the ruin that missionaries have brought to us. What he wrote is called 'The Bottle Imp' and it is about a demon in a bottle which grants its possessor whatever he wishes. But where is that bottle now? There is no sign of it in the house that has become a museum. We believe that this Stevenson took this bottle with him to his grave.'

Keola fell silent and looked across at me. After a long silence I said, 'So now you have men digging to find the bottle?'

'You are a clever man, mister. A very clever man. Yes. That is what we do.'

'But won't the authorities stop you? What about the police? You might be arrested.'

Keola pointed to one of his companions who was sitting on the stump of a felled palm tree and mopping his brow.

'That is my friend, Rangi. He is the police. When we find the bottle we will share the wishes. There will be wishes for all my friends.' He was silent for a moment. Then a thought struck him, 'You can be my friend also. You and your lovely missus may have wishes too. If you are nice to me.' He paused again. 'There is an awful lot of digging and it is dangerous too because of the weight of the concrete overhead. In three days my men are sure that they will be able to bring the body out, but we will not do it in daytime. It will be better to do this at night so as not to attract attention. Then we will take the bottle from this Stevenson, who being dead, will not refuse us, and then we go back down to my house and we all make wishes. Plenty of wishes for everyone. If you are happy, I will come for you early on Thursday evening and you will come with me and my friends and you will see that it is true that he was buried with his magic bottle. The labourers are costing me a fortune. Most of them don't know what we are looking for, though some guess it might gold.'

'I looked at Sylvie. She looked apprehensive and she was right to be so. Nevertheless, I told Keola that we would join the proposed nocturnal expedition. I did not care for this man and I thought that it might be amusing to watch his face when no magic bottle was found in the grave. Apia was short of nighttime entertainments.'

Lancelyn had not noticed that Sylvie had reappeared and was standing beside him and now she interrupted, 'Damn right, I was apprehensive.'

Lancelyn nodded and continued, 'On the Thursday as the dusk was coming on Keola and six of his friends called for us at our hotel. They were also accompanied by one of the seashore sorcerers in case some kind of protective spell might be needed during the exhumation of Stevenson. Also Keola was wearing a necklace of human teeth for good luck. As we entered the dark forest, Keola and Rangi switched on their torches while the other five lit flaming brands. During the ascent Keola and his friends talked noisily, mostly in Samoan, and perhaps this was to keep the bad spirits of the forest away. When we reached the tomb, the team of diggers were ready and waiting to bring out the coffin from under the tomb. Ugly vapours were in the air. Did they come from the tomb? The flaming torches were forced into the earth around the opening of the grave. Now everybody was very quiet while the coffin was levered out and the claws of hammers were used to open it. The seashore sorcerer was at the ready in case his services should be needed. There was the skeleton of the famous author, incongruously attired in shirt, trousers and brown leather shoes and, resting between bony fingers, there was indeed a bottle. The skull was grinning as if it had just enjoyed a good drink. Rangi stepped forward and snatched the bottle from the skeletal hand which fell to pieces as he did so. He passed the bottle to Keola who told the diggers to close the coffin, replace it under the tomb and begin the work of filling in the excavation. Since I had not believed in the existence of the bottle and had only come along for a lark, I was stupefied.

'As we began our walk down to Keola's house, he told us that the diggers and the sorcerer were well paid, "too bloody well paid", and that they had been told that it was a bottle of a very rare and expensive wine that had been rescued from the grave. Then he and his company began to sing some Samoan songs and they tried to teach Sylvie and me to sing along with them. As I looked up through the palm fronds at the stars, I thought that this was what a somewhat hackneyed writer might describe as a "magical moment", but was it possible that it was only the prelude to a powerful manifestation of real magic?

'Keola's house was a shabby two-roomed affair. The bottle was placed on the middle of a table. Then Keola placed a chair in front of the bottle and stretched out his hand to stroke it muttering as he did so. Then the rest took turns in the chair and stroked the bottle as they made their wishes. Nothing happened. From where I stood, it looked as though the bottle was filled with smoke and, though there might have been something glowing within the smoke, this may have been a trick of the lighting. We waited for something to happen and nothing did. Finally one of the men suggested that perhaps the bottle had to be opened and then a demon would emerge and, because he would be grateful to be let out of the bottle, he would grant all of our wishes. The bottle was tightly corked. Another of the men ran back to his house to fetch a corkscrew. While we waited, Keola came up to us and asked, "Why did you not make a wish?"

"I have nothing to wish for. And you?"

He gave me a broad grin.

"I wish for your Sylvie."

Was this some awkward gallantry?

"Sylvie stays with me," I said.

"You will be dead."

Not gallantry then. Keola turned away. The bottle had been uncorked and a column of black smoke rose up to the ceiling and then slowly began to spread across it. Noises accompanied the smoke and, as more and more smoke poured upwards, one could hear that the noises were of two men who seemed to be arguing. At first I thought that they were arguing in a language that was unfamiliar to me and it was a while before I picked out certain names, "Adam", "Archie" and "Kirstie" and I realised that I was listening to a very broad version of the Lowland Scots dialect. Then a third voice came in which was also Scots, but more anglicised and modulated. As I have already told you, I am not as clever as I used to be and it took me fully twenty minutes of listening to the strange din in a darkened room before I realised that what I was listening to was Stevenson's *Weir of Hermiston* and moreover it was that part of the novel which Stevenson had been unable to finish before he died. Archie was engaged in a row with his father, the "hanging judge" Adam Weir and proclaiming his love for Kirstie. So was it conceivable that there was a tiny tape recorder inside the bottle and that it was playing part of a BBC radio dramatisation of *Weir Hermiston*? No, of course not. There I was in this tropical hovel, transfixed, as I struggled to follow this dark and unwritten Scottish romance on the theme of sexuality as a man's fate.

'However I was the only person in Keola's house who had a clue what the voices meant. Sylvie was terrified and now arguments were breaking out among the men. Though none of their wishes had been granted, a bottle full of talking demons had to be worth a lot of money in any market and now, as the room steadily filled with darkness, a fight broke out over the bottle, literally so. Sylvie grabbed me by the hand and she had to drag me to the door. The last thing we heard as we hurried out into the street was the sound of breaking glass.'

Lancelyn paused for dramatic effect.

'Then I awoke and found it was all a dream.'

Another pause.

'No, it was not. This really happened and it was the second time that the completion of a masterpiece of literature had been lost. Sylvie can confirm the truth of all that we experienced. We ran to the hotel. The following morning we sought out the crew and told them that enough of the careening had been done and we would set sail for somewhere later that day if possible. The crew were delighted to be leaving Apia so soon and that afternoon we sailed out of the harbour.'

'Ever since we got here, he has been telling that story to anyone who will listen,' said Sylvie.

Lancelyn patted her hand indulgently.

'Sylvie is not a great conversationalist, but I like the

company here at the club. We mostly talk about sailing and the foreign parts and perils we have faced, even if no one has a yarn as strange as mine.'

Sylvie, who had been looking very bored, walked off, presumably heading for the loo. Lancelyn waited until she was out of earshot. Then, 'I have had it with intellectuals. You are not an intellectual are you, Mr Byrne?

'I'm a warehouseman.'

Lancelyn looked puzzled, but said, 'Good for you.' And after a pause, 'Then how do you come to know Molly?'

'We met at an encounter group.'

'I suppose that's some kind of dating agency. No, don't bother to tell me. Have you read her novel?'

'I only skimmed it. I'm afraid that I'm not much of a one for reading novels.'

'Oh I rather liked it. Very Molly. Lots of sex and energy. When I was younger I used to read what is classified as serious fiction, stuff written by the "pointy heads", and I revelled in detecting the games that writers played with words and plots, but I'm past that now. Admittedly I don't normally read historical fiction. I prefer crime novels. I recently read Patricia Highsmith's *The Talented Mr Ripley*. Damn clever. This Ripley is a real villain, but my heart was in my mouth lest his deceits should be exposed and he should be arrested and sentenced to death for murder. But in general, I find that being clever takes all the fun out of reading. It's no good beginning a detective novel and guessing almost from the outset how the murder was done and how the murderer will be caught.'

Then looking over his shoulder lest Sylvie might already be returning, 'How do you make a blonde laugh on a Saturday?'

Pause. 'Tell her a joke on Wednesday.' He laughed at his own joke before continuing, 'Stupidity is really preferable to beauty, because beauty fades, but with Sylvie I am blessed with both. No, but seriously, when I was a young man I had all sorts of strange ambitions and fears, but now that I am somewhat older, I have come to realise that only one thing in life matters and that is to have as much sex as possible before one dies. My best hope is to die while experiencing the peak of an orgasm — what is known as the *mors justi.*'

Now Sylvie was back and Lancelyn changed the subject once again and asked Tom, 'I have been thinking of taking the yacht up to Fife and revisiting old haunts. That reminds me. Did Molly visit me in hospital?'

Sylvie answered for him, 'I visited you in hospital. The bitch didn't.'

Lancelyn ignored this and turning to Tom, 'Sylvie, bless her, blames Molly for driving me mad, but it wasn't Molly. It was my strange books that did that to me. I became frightened of them. They wanted too much of me. Then the madness was something I needed to go through in order to emerge healed and stronger. Well, that's just about it. Sylvie and I usually nap after lunch. I do grant Molly absolution, by the way. I sound like a pope saying that. Perhaps I might add my blessing. Beauty does have its privileges. Is she still beautiful?'

Tom nodded before rising and thanking him for lunch. Sylvie saw Tom out of the clubhouse and dismissed him with these words,

'I wish that you had not come. It just stirs up horrid things from the past. Do not think of ever trying to see us again.'

As he made his way to the ferry, Tom wondered if

Lancelyn could possibly have been be telling the truth about what happened in Samoa. Or was it that Lancelyn was still insane and Sylvie had joined him in this, making a *folie à deux*? Whatever the truth of the matter, it was strange stuff to have to listen to in a yacht club. Molly rang him the following evening, wanting to know everything. Was she forgiven? How was Lancelyn? What did he look like? Where had he been? Was he with anyone? Tom told her that she was forgiven, but that she would have to wait for their tryst in the warehouse in order to learn more. That would be on the coming Saturday when he would be on night duty.

CHAPTER FIFTEEN

But it was on Tuesday that something else happened. He had negotiated a longer than usual lunchbreak and he was hurrying along past the headquarters of the British Interplanetary Society on South Lambeth Road and intending to do some shopping at the Oval, when he almost collided with a man coming out of the building. The man's face was familiar, but the meeting was so unexpected that at first Tom could not place him. Finally he said, 'Bernard, do you remember me? We met in a pub in Oxford?'

'Of course I remember you. What on earth are you doing here?'

'I work nearby in Nine Elms.'

'I work here. I don't have much time. I have just come out for some fresh air. Is Nine Elms where the headquarters of the bodyguarding services are?'

'I'm a warehouseman. What about you?'

'I hope you don't mind me saying so, but "warehouseman" sounds less exciting. Still I dare say it is code for "bodyguard". As for me, I think I told you that I was going to try the Society for Psychical Research, but they said that they had no interest in taking on an expert on fictional ghosts. They were only interested in real ghosts — as if there were such things. But then I thought that I would have another go in locating Cassie and the rest of the Bradbury Institute in America. I found out that the British Interplanetary Society is sort of affiliated with NASA. So I turned up here to make enquiries and maybe be put in touch with the relevant persons in NASA. NASA is such a huge organisation. I got to talking with the boss here. He did not know anything about the Bradbury Institute, but, as I talked, he was struck by how much I seemed to know about Mars. And it's true. Having spent so much time with the astrophysicist, the astronomers and the rest in Newcastle, as well having read so much and looked at all those maps, I do know a huge amount about Mars. I kept on talking about what I knew regarding Mars until I was offered a job.

'The British Interplanetary Society promotes the exploration and use of space for the benefit of humanity and it seeks to inspire and advance knowledge in all aspects of aeronautics. Once I got to grips with the work here, it occurred to me to apply the Ignatian method, or rather *The Spiritual Exercises of Saint Ignatius of Loyola* to the study of Martian topography. The first point is to see with the eyes of the imagination the iron-oxide-red and the hellish landscape with its gigantic dead volcanoes, treacherous chasms, jets of methane and billowing dust storms. The second, to hear with the ears the howling of the solar winds and crunching of my feet on the endless and toxic salt sands of Mars. The third, to smell with the sense of smell the sulphurous foul vapours which drift in the thin air over the surface of the planet. The fourth, to taste with the taste of bitter things, the desolation of its empty places. The fifth, to feel its lethal chills and scorching heats. So, if I persist, I may possibly make a colloquy with Christ Our Lord, and bring to memory the Martians who once dwelt on that hellish planet and it may even be that at the end of my extra-terrestrial journeying I shall encounter Christ, as I believe Raven did.'

Now Tom wanted to tell Bernard what he had learned from Molly and Mortimer about Raven and about Lancelyn, but it was all rather complicated and meanwhile Bernard continued, 'On the other hand, it may well be that the hellish landscape of Mars has nothing to offer in the way of spiritual solace. Nevertheless, the work is most absorbing and my skill at mapping out in convincing detail the topography of the planet has made me a valued member of the Society. We are beginning to plan for a grand research project, provisionally entitled Project Boreas, which will seek to assess the practicability of establishing a manned station at the Martian North Pole where, decades from now, the scientists assigned to the station will conduct a quest for water and habitable conditions. My current project is to head a virtual exploration of the Boreal Chasm, a 350-mile-long canyon within the polar ice cap. Since the ice cap is plunged in perpetual darkness, it is challenging stuff.

'Of course it is nothing like the Bradbury Institute. The staff here are mostly men. As for the Bradbury Institute:

"*That was the land of lost content,*
I see it shining plain,
The happy highways where I went
And cannot come again."

I'm glad we met and we must meet again soon. But this is an exceptionally busy week and my few minutes' break are up. Look in sometime next week and we can arrange a proper time for a meeting in a pub and you can tell me more about yourself and bodyguard work and, of course, Molly. Does she still need a bodyguard? Now it occurs to me that I may be a bit slow on the uptake. I am not up-to-date with contemporary slang and I dare say that both "bodyguard" and "warehouseman" are slang terms for "lover". Don't answer that now. Come and look me up here sometime next week and we can go off and have lunch in a pub.'

With that Bernard went back indoors and Tom hastened his pace towards the Oval.

When Saturday evening came round Molly arrived at the Nine Elms warehouse, dressed as if for a fashion shoot, wearing a long tangerine and yellow dress and a turban. As it happened, this particular warehouse was often used for fashion shoots by photographers who wanted a gritty masculine background to their portraits of stylishly dressed, bored-looking young women. The warehouse had also hosted the makers of feature films and television dramas who had to have the perfectly clichéd setting for that culminating gunfight between gangsters.

Tom helped Molly bring in the rugs and cushions from the taxi. Molly was apologetic about the gun. Marcus had found the one that they had been using and confiscated it. She had rung Ferdie and, at short notice, begged him for a replacement.

'This was the best that he could do.'

They looked at the gun dubiously. It looked like a cross between a sawn-off shotgun and an antiquated handgun.

There was no safety catch. Tom wanted to show her round the warehouse immediately, but Molly wanted sex first and, once they had got the rugs and cushions down in one of the empty palette areas, she handed the gun to him. The absence of a safety catch gave an added intensity to their coupling. Afterwards he took her by the hand and they walked, naked as Adam and Eve, in this dimly-lit industrial paradise, which also served as a cathedral of the service economy. Tom explained how access to the loading bays was secured, how goods were cross-docked, how the pick and pack process worked, how inventories also served as maps to the locations of the items that were required and finally he switched on a horizontal carousel for her to admire. She seemed fascinated. With this beautiful woman beside him, Tom asked himself was this to be the crowning moment of his life? Surely a happiness as intense as this could never ever be repeated.

When a thing is complete, it begins to fall apart. Occasionally he heard rustling and he resolved that tomorrow he would report to the manager that rats had once again made their way into their industrial paradise. Before that he would have to give Molly a full account of what he had learned at Cowes. As they returned to the empty palette area where the cushions, rugs and a bottle of wine were, she said, 'My turn with the gun.'

She started rummaging among the blankets.

'What did you do with it? Where is the gun?'

Another voice replied, 'Here.'

Then, 'What a sight! You certainly know how to give a girl a good time.'

The loud voice echoed through the warehouse. With that,

a man emerged from the shadows. A long black coat hung over his shoulders. It had to be Jaimie. His right arm was in a sling and the gun was held in his left hand.

'Don't mind me. If you do want to screw again, then carry on. I have enjoyed watching. But then, Molly, darling, I want you back in Scotland. He, whoever he is, can come too. I'm not jealous. I only follow you to make sure you are safe, but I can't always be down in London. Back in St Andrews, you can be safe with me and we can set up house together. Like old times. We were once happy. Now I am so desperate for you that I would rather die than leave without you.'

He raised the gun and then paused for a moment and looked at it as if baffled by its appearance. Tom, who being naked was feeling definitely vulnerable, nevertheless advanced on him, saying, 'Hand me the gun and no one gets hurt. If not, I will break your other wrist.'

Jaimie looked terrified, but he raised the gun the gun higher and said, 'Don't come any nearer or I will shoot.'

Tom took a step closer. Jaimie raised the gun and, pointing at his own head, he pulled the trigger. There was no sound. Then a small white banner dropped down from the barrel of the gun. On it in big red letters was the word 'BANG!' Jaimie looked at the banner for a moment, before he dropped the gun and gave a half sob. Then he hastened towards the warehouse's exit. Tom started to laugh, but, when he looked behind him, he could see that Molly's eyes were moist with tears. They got dressed and he went to the manager's office and phoned for a taxi to take Molly back to Highgate.

'That was fun!' she said, though the look on her face suggested that the final confrontation had been no fun at all.

Tom said, 'Let's get outta here!'

He saw her to the taxicab and went back to stand in front of the warehouse doors and waited for it to drive off. As it began to move off, he saw Jaimie come out from behind some bushes and the cab abruptly stopped and Tom watched as Molly opened the door for Jaimie to clamber in. That was the end of everything. He would never tell Molly about the things that he had heard from Lancelyn, or about his second encounter with Bernard. The following morning Tom turned up at the warehouse, but only to hand in his resignation. He would:

> '...*arise now and go to Innisfree.*
> *And a small cabin build there.*'

Not literally Innisfree. That was Yeats. For Tom, it had to be Cashel.

CHAPTER SIXTEEN

Looking back on his last night at the warehouse, perhaps it was right for Molly to let Jaimie join her in her in the taxicab, for it might be that Jaimie, in his weird way, had loved her more than he had done. He also harboured a faint suspicion that Molly and Ferdie had set the whole thing up and so the business in the warehouse could have been a mini-drama and maybe even Jaimie was part of it too. Molly was what Yeats might have called 'a terrible beauty'. It was all too difficult to think about.

Once Tom was back in Cashel, there was a meeting with Maeve in a teahouse. Of course it should have been on Cashel Mount, but it was raining quite hard and then, if he had knelt before her in the teahouse, people might have thought that he was about to propose to her. He had no intention of doing that. Anyway Maeve seemed happy enough with the teahouse. Her hair was swept back in a bun and its brilliant red had faded to a light copper colour and there were even a few streaks of silvery white in it. Having grown used to Molly's flamboyant displays of couture, he found Maeve's costume dowdy. More disturbing yet, there was now a grannyish timbre to her voice. She had lost her regal air and just seemed pitifully eager to please. Not regal, more clingy. He judged that she must be the victim of a tragically premature and accelerating ageing process.

> '*O who could have foretold*
> *That the heart grows old.*'

The meeting had to be got through. He talked about his work at the warehouse and about his no-good volumes of poetry. He also talked in very general terms about his vague plans for a verse drama and how that had come to nothing. But he did not mention Molly or anyone associated with her. Now he was back in Cashel, he would find work of some kind and see how things went. Maeve spoke a bit about her earlier ambition to become a dancer. Nothing had come of that.

A little later, when Tom looked back on that meeting in the teahouse and then compared it to their previous confrontation on Mount Cashel, he wept. This was the damage wrought by time. This was life. He found work in the local supermarket as a shelf stacker. Though this was a comedown from warehousing, it was nevertheless quite absorbing and he was good at it. He was good at getting impulse purchases displayed near the exit and ensuring that canned goods were normally placed on the lower shelves. He made sure that stock was ready in reserve in order to fill the gaps left by the morning and evening rush hour purchases. He was assiduous in getting go-backs returned to their proper places on the shelves and he found it easy to hold in his head the sums paid by certain manufacturers in order to have their branded goods given more space. Within a couple of months he had been promoted to be the supermarket's stock manager. Even so, the quasi-mathematical beauty of the warehouse was not there.

He put all thoughts of writing poetry behind him. He now thought that one had to be really clever in order to be a poet. It would also have helped if he had had a more interesting life. Also modern poetry must be difficult. Most poets, most artists, most novelists are failures. So there was nothing special about Tom. But perhaps there is poetry in failure, just as there is beauty in melancholy. Moreover, with regard to the sorts of things that he wanted to say, it always turned out that Yeats had been there before him. Yeats was like the weather, impossible to walk away from. He recited Yeats to himself:

> '*And I shall have peace*
> *For the peace comes dropping slow.*'

So now Tom was off the noisy, colourful and rapidly revolving Carousel of Adventure. Heroes are not changed by their adventures, not at least while those adventures are going on. Hercules was the same man after he completed his seven labours as he was before he started. The same with Galahad on his quest for the Holy Grail. Hornblower did not change as he advanced from midshipman to rear admiral. But Tom, no hero, had been changed by his ride on the Carousel. For better or worse, he now knew his limits. Probably Lancelyn was right that the main thing in life was to have as much sex as possible. But grand passion could never return. Though stock management kept him busy, his nights were frightful. Again and again he dreamt of guns, conjuring tricks, car chases, burials, disinterments, Martian landscapes and Molly. The same elements kept finding new ways to arrange themselves in his nightmares. Molly, Quentin, Lancelyn, Jaimie, Bernard and Mortimer talked to him in his sleep, but they were all talking about a book that he had not read.

He went to evening classes in Irish country dancing and there he met Erin. Three months later they were married. A month after that they bought a television. In the evenings they went dancing or watched programmes like the Eurovision Song Contest, The Riordans and Wanderly Wagon. He told Erin as little as possible about his time in London. And, yes, Lancelyn had been right about the meaning of life.

> *'But a coarse old man am I,*
> *I chose the second-best, I forget it all awhile*
> *Upon a woman's breast.'*

Yeats notwithstanding, second-best was still pretty good. Tom no longer had visions of fairies in gusts of wind or street-corner thimbleriggers. The fairies do not like the advance of age and they shun it. Tom did not miss them. He and Erin had children, a boy and a girl. After the children had been seen off to university, Tom took early retirement.

So it was that when Mortimer came for Tom, he found him at home. Though Tom reluctantly let him in and Erin offered him tea, for it was teatime, Mortimer demanded whisky. It was just like Tom's last meeting with him and Mortimer was not to be denied. Though he smiled at Erin, she looked terrified and Tom's hand shook as he poured out the whisky.

'How did you find me?'

'Molly told me that you were originally from this place.

Once here, it just took me a bit of legwork and asking around to track you down.'

'Why are you here? Does *The Times Literary Supplement* want to interview me under the heading of "A Strangely Neglected Irish Poet?"'

'I no longer work for *The Times Literary Supplement*. I am bringing you an invitation from Sir Marcus Wainwright to attend a weekend-long grand reception at his country house outside Cheltenham.'

'Who is this Wainwright?'

'I am sure you must have read about him in the newspapers. He is the grand television executive, probably the grandest of them all — and Molly must often have mentioned him.'

'Oh, that Marcus. What is the celebration for and why does he need me at it?'

Mortimer hesitated, 'Molly is now his wife. She told me that she would like to see you. The reception is not exactly a celebration, though there will be drinks, fireworks and a conjuring show. But the main purpose of a select gathering is to listen to the second of Edward Raven's tapes. Charles and I want everybody who heard the first recorded message to be present to hear the second one.'

'I don't understand. What has Marcus to do with any of this? I am pretty sure that he was not present at the playing of the first recording. What is more I have never had any particular interest in Raven or his strange teaching technique.'

'True, I suppose. But Molly and Marcus were friends at Oxford and now she is his wife and Molly is central to what is planned. On the day after the playing of the tape, she and Ferdinand Harris, or the Great Zamboni as he is more commonly known, want everybody to assemble in what they are calling an "encounter group" in order to explore the meaning of the two tapes, as well as the web of connections between Molly, Lancelyn and Bernard and those who knew them. In some mysterious way it all seems to be connected. You did listen to the first tape. You were in the same "encounter group" as Molly and Ferdinand. You have met Lancelyn, Bernard and Jaimie. So, quite unwittingly, you have become part of our story.'

'I'm me. I'm not part of your story. I don't want to see Molly again and I am staying here in Cashel, where the people aren't all mad, but just ordinary.'

Mortimer produced a notebook from his pocket and made a series of jottings before replying, 'That would be most regrettable. If you are really sure, then I will waste no more of my time or yours and report back to Sir Marcus. He needs to be told as soon as possible. I hope that you do not come to regret this.'

'Go.'

But then Erin, looking scared but determined, put up her hand, 'No. Stay,' and, turning to Tom, 'I want you to go. I think you need to see these people. I will be fine on my own. Please darling. What you need is to finish whatever was started in London.'

Tom shook his head.

'Please darling.'

Tom stared at Mortimer who stared implacably back. Then he looked once more to Erin, before he finally agreed to accept Marcus's invitation. Mortimer said that the reception would be held in little over a month's time, beginning on the

18th of June. Tom would shortly receive confirmation by a formal invitation together with additional information. A car would take him to Dublin airport and there would be another car waiting for him at Heathrow. With that, Mortimer again wrote something in the notebook, before thanking his hosts for the whisky and leaving.

Once he had gone, Tom and Erin abandoned their cups of tea and poured themselves whisky.

'What a strange man! He looked more like a thug than a literary editor.'

'I guess lots of literary editors are like that. How is that you are so keen to see me off?'

'It is not like that. I wish you weren't going, but I think that you really have to. It may be a kind of exorcism that will be good for you.'

'I have never said much or anything about my last year in London. Those people that Mortimer mentioned, you don't know what they were like and I don't want to tell you.'

'And I don't want to know. But sometimes you talk in your sleep. Besides, of late, there has been a strange look in your eyes. I can't describe it, but it is a bit like the eyes of Frodo in that *Lord of the Rings* film which we saw. I want you to come back to me cured of whatever it is.'

CHAPTER SEVENTEEN

The car came early on the appointed day. Tom hugged and kissed Erin before clambering into what felt like his hearse. There was another car waiting at Heathrow and it delivered him to Marcus's mansion in time for pre-dinner drinks. They were a select gathering at dinner: Marcus, Molly, Charles, Edward and Tom. Molly greeted him formally and introduced him to the rest. Other guests would be arriving later that night or in the course of the following day.

Molly had aged of course, but, unlike Maeve, there was nothing grannyish about her. She was regal and, though a little plump, she was still desirable. As for Tom, he used to look like Robert Redford in *Barefoot in the Park*. Now he was so much older, he still looked like Redford, but it was Redford in *The Horse Whisperer*. Marcus might possibly once have been handsome, but he was now red-eyed and fat. He talked about television celebrities who had promised that they would come. He also drank heavily and he kept scribbling notes at the table since he was fretting about the speech he must make on the following day. Charles, who had moved from the Pentagon to advising the State Department, looked unchanged since Tom had heard him speak in Oxford all those years ago, except that his hair had turned steel-grey. Edward, the man who had been something at the German Central Bank in Frankfurt, had recently retired to Farnborough where he was busy with the collecting and cultivation of rare orchids. He talked at boring length about his plants. Molly, in order to change the subject, asked Charles about his flight. Then she thought to ask him about the saint he had mentioned in his speech at Raven's funeral, the saint who was supposed to be the patron saint of air travellers. Was he perhaps some exceptionally pious Alitalia pilot?

'Indeed no. Saint Joseph of Cupertino was a seventeenth-century Italian Franciscan and he took flight without any assistance from the aviation industry. From the first he was a clumsy, stupid and inattentive youth and then later he was carelessly prone to briefly taking to the air. As often as not he took off while on his knees in front of the altar during celebration of the Mass. But a prayer, the sound of church bells, a holy icon or the name of the Blessed Virgin might also be sufficient to set him aloft. After shrieking out and then fainting from ecstasy and still unconscious he would rise up backwards into the air.

He did not need to be in church to take off. "He flew similarly from an olive tree and there remained in a kneeling posture for the space of half an hour. A marvellous thing it was to see the branch which sustained him swaying lightly, as though a bird had landed upon it." Sometimes people would have to help him get back to the ground by pulling him down. In the course of his life he levitated thousands of times and hundreds of people witnessed these manifestations of the miraculous. Sometimes he carried a terrified bystander aloft. On one occasion a noble lunatic was brought to him and seizing the lunatic by the hair he held him up in the air for a quarter of hour before returning him to earth, by which time the nobleman was cured of his insanity. Apart from just the flying, those who saw Joseph aloft marvelled that his robes never caught fire from the candles around or on the altar, as well as his ability when he sometimes landed on the altar to avoid disturbing any of the objects which might be displayed there.

'At first it was feared that his levitations might be manifestations of witchcraft and consequently he was investigated by the Inquisition. Nevertheless his piety and austerity could not be denied and, for example, he ate solid food only twice a week. His levitations were often distracting for others who had come to worship and these showy miracles were widely disapproved of. So eventually he was confined to his cell like a prisoner. Yet this could not dim his joy in all that was holy — and everything was holy. As I say, he was a stupid and inattentive man and therefore he has also become the patron saint of those with mental handicaps. Joseph's miracles were so widely and frequently attested that a sceptical interpretation along the lines that that he was good at jumping or that those who saw him levitate were subject to mass hypnosis are so ridiculous that it is actually more rational, more logical to accept the existence of the supernatural and its origins in the Divine — a matter of Occam's razor. It must be admitted that miracles are fearful things to behold and they may even be an obstacle to one's offering the correct worship that is God's due. Joseph's levitations were the extreme product of ecstasy and ecstasy can be a terrible thing, as I know to my cost.'

No one knew what to say to this. Commiserate with Charles? Check what miracles he had seen? Attempt to rebut his stuff about the supernatural and Occam's razor? Find out how ecstasy differed from just feeling very happy? Query whether levitation was a particularly Catholic thing? So instead the dinner-table conversation moved on with Molly enthusing about the novels she had published after *The Rod and The Knout*. They included one on Boadicea and another on a lady pirate and they were close to bestsellers. Yet another one on Semiramis was forthcoming.

Everybody except Tom had made a success of their lives. He could not decide whether to blame Molly or Yeats for his failure. Molly plied him with questions about Erin. There was an unspoken understanding that they would not discuss the serious business of the following days, whatever that might be. Lancelyn, Sylvie, Bernard, Ferdie and Jaimie were all expected to arrive by the following morning. When he heard these names, he wondered how it could be that Molly was married to Marcus and yet Bernard would be coming. After dinner, before retiring, he took Molly aside and quietly asked about Bernard. He did not dare use the word 'bigamy'.

'Oh didn't you read about it in the papers? It was quite a sensation at the time. Eventually Bernard was easy to track down. Charles was put in contact with him at the British Interplanetary Society by NASA and then there was a great deal of faff and some expense while Bernard and I secured an amiable divorce before Marcus and I went through a second wedding ceremony. Bernard is terribly grand these days. He is Britain's leading expert on the planet Mars. He has published books and made a documentary series for television and he is a Fellow of the Royal Society.'

Tom reflected gloomily on another bloody success story as he made his way to bed.

The following morning when Tom came down to breakfast he found Ferdie helping himself to the kedgeree. Ferdie had arrived late last night and then he had had to supervise the unloading of equipment before the tiger was given its final feed. The tiger?

'Yes, it is a white Siberian tiger. It gets through the most enormous quantities of meat. Also there is always a certain amount of paperwork to be done. He has to be transported in a double enclosure. The aluminium inner crate is enormously heavy. It takes six people to move it and requires a reinforced trailer. But he is certainly worth his weight in steaks. His presence on stage adds adrenaline to the act. My audiences are afraid for me and for themselves. But he is just a great big overfed pussycat and we love each other. I call him Snookins.'

Tom had noticed that Ferdie, who was now bald and looking horribly gaunt, was having difficulty with his kedgeree. This was probably because he no longer had any teeth. The bad breath was as fierce as ever. Outside in the fresh air Tom watched servants carrying out tables, chairs and napery to the big marquee. Mortimer, whom Tom had noticed talking earnestly to Molly at breakfast, was now also outside, pacing around the grounds and occasionally making jottings in a notebook. Tom wondered what he did these days. Was he perhaps acting as Marcus' security or his factotum? Horses were taken out to exercise, peacocks strutted about and, as the early morning hours passed, the strutting birds were joined by people. Lots of these strutting people looked as though they expected to be recognised because they made regular appearances on television, but since Tom watched only a select number of Irish programmes he did not succeed in recognising any of them.

Then, spotting Charles among the gathering throng, Tom went over and asked him about the second tape. What would it contain? What had Raven's intention been when making it? Charles shrugged.

'Perhaps we shall learn the Meaning of Life, or if not the Meaning of Life, at least the meaning of our lives. Raven was a remarkable man. But at times I have found myself wondering if it will not turn out to be the case that there is nothing very much on the second tape and that its real purpose was to bring his favourite former students and related persons together once more. The other possibility, of course, is that the tape will contain his confession of his paedophile and convict past and his reinvention as an eccentric teacher of English Literature.'

Then Tom wanted to know what Charles had found out about the Bradbury Institute. Had it indeed been affiliated with NASA?

'No. NASA knew nothing about it and they were most concerned when I told them what little I knew. Institutional impersonation can be a serious offence. So I then passed the problem on to the CIA. We have been giving a lot of thought to this. I know that back in the 70s the Russians were big in psychical research and they investigated the potential usefulness to warfare and espionage of such things as telepathy, teleportation, clairvoyance and precognition. My best guess is that the Institute in Newcastle was a front for Soviet scholars who were researching interplanetary ghosts.'

Tom did not think that this was at all likely and decided to ask Bernard what he thought about this theory. His own suspicion was that Bernard had made the whole thing up. Charles walked off to consult with Edward about something.

Tom now set out to find Bernard, but he came across Lancelyn first. Lancelyn, who was leaning on a stick, had just encountered Molly. Tom did not wish to get close to Molly and so he did not join them, but stood close enough to listen and he was immediately joined by Sylvie, whose loathing for Molly was obvious. But Lancelyn was genial in a disturbingly vague way.

'Molly Ransom! How wonderful to see you again! I had thought that you were dead. I was sure you had committed suicide, though why you should have wished to commit suicide I cannot think. I believe I read about it in a newspaper. Or perhaps it was the poet who committed suicide.'

Sylvie muttered to Tom, 'He never reads newspapers. He only buys *The Times* for the crossword.'

And Molly, who looked as though she wished she was somewhere else, replied, 'I think what it is that you are remembering is the ending of my first novel, *The Rod and the Knout*, at the end of which both Natasha and the poet who was her lover commit suicide.'

'Ah yes, that must be it. The gloomily soulful poet was a memorable creation. Just too good for this world. I do enjoy a good romance, whereas everything is about sex these days. Did you know that I have been mentally castrated by electro-convulsive therapy? These days I am an intellectual eunuch, the sort who takes two hours to do *The Times Crossword*.'

At this point Sylvie muttered to Tom, 'But he's got sex

coming out of his ears.'

'What did you say, darling?'

'I said that no one expects tears.'

Then she added in a lower voice to Tom, 'That is why he is a bit deaf.'

Molly, who was looking desperate, asked, 'Apart from the ECT and the walking stick, are you well, Lancelyn?'

'Mustn't grumble. Sylvie and I have been travelling about on our yacht. Where is Sylvie? Ah, there she is. Say hello to Molly, Sylvie. While we were in Samoa the strangest thing happened. You will want to hear this…'

Molly was now frantically signalling to someone in the distance. It was Bernard, who was having an animated conversation with Quentin, and they both walked over to join Molly and Lancelyn.

'Hello Molly,' said Bernard. 'It has been a long time. You look well. Do you know Quentin? He and I have been exchanging words. I have given him "ichnites", the term used to designate the traces left by dinosaurs, and Quentin has given me "fulginochronology" which means the study of ancient soot. Do you have a word for us?'

She ignored this and turning to Lancelyn, she said, 'This is Bernard,' she said. 'You remember him, don't you?'

'I remember a Bernard. We used to do crosswords together.'

'I am that Bernard,' he said.

'His memory these days is pathetic,' said Sylvie.

'What was that dear?'

'I said these days we're peripatetic.'

'Ah! Bernard really? You don't look like him. But I dare

say that there is more than one Bernard. Well, Bernard, if you insist, are you still in the business of analysing ghost stories?'

'I have moved on to a more fruitful area of enquiry and I have made myself an expert on the topography and geology of Mars.'

'The topography of Mars is no laughing matter. What is the big smile for, Bernard?' Molly wanted to know.

'I just heard this morning that All Souls wants me back, this time as a professor. Since the failure of the Beagle 2 landing craft, I shall have a lot of work to do, as I will certainly be involved in the attempt to locate its crash site. But I think I may also do a course of lectures on the gravitational pull of Mars on the British imagination. The Edgar Rice Burroughs novels, the *Dan Dare* comic strip in the *Eagle*, *Journey into Space* on the radio, C. S. Lewis' *Out of the Silent Planet*. Things like that. It strikes me now that Mars romances are really for the young. For most adults the planet is a useless rocky sphere. We are so lonely in our solar system. I am sure that the Martians, lonely too, were waiting for us, but the Mars Express came too late, four billion years too bloody late. Well the Martians should not have expected the early hominids to be able to use their fire sticks and flint stones to construct a spaceship.'

Tom wondered if All Souls had been running short of mad professors. Turning away from Bernard, Lancelyn said to Quentin, 'Of course, I remember you, Quentin. You were in the History Department. And I see that you, like me and Tom here, have become dependent on a walking stick.'

'Yes indeed, and since acquiring my first walking stick, I have become quite the rhabdophilist.'

'Rabdowhat?'

'A rhabdophilist is a person who collects sticks or is an enthusiast for them.'

'Rhabdophilist ought to mean someone who gets sexual pleasure from walking sticks.'

'Well, I believe there are people known as disability pretenders, some of these denizens of the Court of Miracles make money or get other kinds of pleasure from pretending that they have lost a limb or something, though that is not the same thing. But pretending to have a disability is a tricky business. I have noticed that actors in films usually get it wrong and have the stick on the same side as the disability, whereas it should be in the hand on the opposite side from the side which needs support. Then the affected leg and the stick should move forward in unison. I have quite a collection of canes now, including a cane topped with a skull, a swordstick, a cane with a tiny flask of whisky set in its head, a crystal dress cane…'

Suddenly Lancelyn shouted, 'Ooporphyrin!'

They all looked at him.

'You wanted a word. "Ooporphyrin" refers to the brown pigment found in eggshells. You are welcome. Now I was about to tell Molly about the most extraordinary occurrence that I witnessed in Samoa…'

'I'm sorry Lancelyn but I have just seen Marcus signalling. I am needed urgently.'

And Molly hurried off in the direction of the marquee. At this point Bernard noticed Tom.

'Ah the bodyguard in the pub! Are you still working as a bodyguard?'

'There is not much call for geriatric bodyguards.'

Bernard was looking over Tom's shoulder, prompting him to ask, 'You are looking for somebody?'

'I was hoping that Cassie might turn up,' Bernard replied. 'You remember me telling you about Cassie all those years ago.'

'Have you met Charles yet? He thinks that Cassie and her team were part of a Russian undercover investigative operation to carry out psychical research in Britain.'

Bernard shook his head, 'Oh no, that won't do. Their American accents and vocabulary were impeccable. And besides why would the Russians set up in Newcastle? No, I have given that time in my life a great deal of thought and it is now my belief that the Bradbury Institute was an outlying province of Fairyland. I don't wonder that you are looking doubtful. Just don't laugh. But, my God, you cannot imagine the things that Cassie got up to in bed. No ordinary woman could have assumed the positions and matched the tricks that Cassie performed. Nowhere near. When I was a callow student I used to argue that Fairyland was just a social construct. Now I am older and wiser. It was a bit of Fairyland masquerading as something else.'

Why would the fairies choose to set up in Newcastle? What was so great about Newcastle? Better not to ask. All Souls did not know what they were getting.

Bernard continued, 'In retrospect I think the Institute had two aims. First, they were not really looking for ghosts, but rather for elfin creatures like themselves on other planets. Secondly, everything had been arranged so as to rescue me from myself. Why I was chosen I cannot guess. Though I hope that Cassie will appear, at the same time, in my heart of hearts,

I know that she will not. Fairies are only for young people.'

And now, when Tom looked round him he could see that Marcus' reception was indeed a kind of dark carnival in which the guests did not need masks, since they were disguised by old age in a grand festival of the ugly and decrepit. Mostly ugly anyway. On the edge of the lawn Tom could see that Ferdie was having a row with a handsome young man in overalls. The row ended with Ferdie slapping the man's face and then walking away in tears.

Quentin who was still standing beside Marcus shrugged and then said to Tom.

'We have met before. You were at the viewing for the auction of Lancelyn's books.'

'Yes, you were a history professor in St Andrews.'

'I am now emeritus. Now that I am retired, I find that at last I have had time to finish and publish my book on the Pilgrimage of Grace.'

Tom was about to ask what this pilgrimage was when Quentin suddenly said, 'Oh dear. Here he comes.'

It was Jaimie and a female companion. Tom guessed that this might be Saffron. Jaimie had at last lost the cherubic appearance that Mortimer and Molly had evoked. He now looked like an aged survivor from an excessively prolonged Roman orgy. More strikingly he now relied on a crutch, since he only had one leg.

Lancelyn was on to this, 'Jaimie! How nice to see you! At least most of you, for I see that you now only have one leg, "whereas the common prejudice runs in favour of two".'

'Hello Lancelyn. Who needs two legs? A few years back I was saying to Saffron how ever since I was a boy I had wanted to be one-legged, just like Long John Silver.'

'That's body dysphoria or apotemnophilia,' said Quentin.

Jaimie looked irritated by the interruption and continued,

'To my surprise she told me that she fancied me as I was, but that she would fancy me even more if I had only one leg.'

'That will be sexual arousal in response to a partner's amputation, better known as acromotophilia, but also known as the love that cannot spell its name.'

It was clear that Jaimie wanted to brain Quentin with his crutch, but was unable to work out how to do it without falling over. So he continued, 'So that was it. We found a suitably quiet stretch of the Dundee-Edinburgh railway line. Saffron rang emergency services even before I put my leg on the line. Naturally the pain was excruciating and I lost a lot of blood, but in the long run it was so worth it. Later we had a bit of a battle with the hospital to reclaim the lost leg, but we won and we had it embalmed. It lies on our mantelpiece. And I feel so much lighter and liberated and the sex is better too.'

Quentin explained to the others, 'The English Department has more than its fair share of eccentrics.'

Plainly there was much to discuss here, but at this point Mortimer strode up and planted himself in front of Jaimie before punching him in the mouth. The crutch went flying and Jamie fell back against Saffron. Blood was streaming down his chin. Quentin fetched his crutch back for him and Jaimie, surprisingly agile, limped swiftly towards the house with Saffron following.

'The Tooth Fairy is going to be busy tonight,' said Mortimer, before making another jotting in his notebook.

Not knowing who might be next to get a punch in the face,

the group backed away from him and dispersed. Tom made his way to the marquee. He needed somewhere to sit and rest. But first he helped himself to some sandwiches and a glass of wine. Marcus was well into his speech and, as Tom rested, he heard Marcus pass on from gloomy prognostications about the future of television to a lament for the disappearance of coal mines and the grassing over of their majestic industrial beauty. For centuries coal mines had been a historic part of the British landscape. Tom would have liked to have stayed and heard more, but it was hard to follow the detail of what Marcus was saying, as the tent was full of people who were not interested in the speech and who were noisily chattering amongst themselves.

It was hardly better outside. Tom walked into a wall of sound.

'But old age, to begin with, has something in common with death. Some face it with indifference, not because they have more courage than others, but because they have less imagination.' 'That does not sound like you.' 'It is from Proust's *Time Regained*.' '*Vita brevis, ars longa*, Proust longer yet.' 'Snookins? The Siberian white tiger, being a variety of the Bengal tiger, usually has obvious black stripes, but Snookins has almost no stripes at all. I bought him as a cub from Cincinnati Zoo.' 'Romantic Ireland is dead and gone. They are with O'Leary in the grave.' 'Then I handed my gun in to the police and we had a good laugh about it.' 'Phalaenopsis orchids are best to start with. They are plentiful and you get a good variety of colours with them. But for my money, and I have plenty of that, nothing can beat Rothschild's slipper orchid with its wonderful reds and golds. It is very rare and, for the rarer orchids imported from abroad, you will need to repot and quarantine them. Failure to do so could easily lead to disaster.' 'You interest me strangely.' 'It is called an iPhone.' 'Catching a bullet between one's teeth is not as difficult as it looks. Obviously I can't do it anymore because I have lost all my teeth. But I could easily show you how. Now where is Rupert?' 'The population under scrutiny is oblivious to the science of psychohistory.' If only his story had been true.' 'If my aunt had had testicles she would have been my uncle.' 'Stick management is the thing.' 'Don't you mean carrot and stick management?' 'No, just the stick. Carrots won't help you at all with your balance. As an additional bonus, my walking stick doubles as a wand for my marvels to perform.' 'Who is that man who says that he is Bernard? I'm sure I know him from somewhere.' 'He was telling me that tiger petting has become quite the thing.' 'We always fry ours in batter.' 'Anybody who has lived through the sixties is likely to be suffering post-traumatic stress disorder.' 'The orchid was one of the earliest flowering plants. They were here before the dinosaurs. What is more, an orchid can live for up to a hundred years. Now I am going to give you the addresses of two of the best garden centres.' 'Molly's bum is bigger. Bigger and better, I'd say.' 'At this point the bottle was unstopped. Black smoke filled the room and voices came out of the darkness. It took me a while to realise that what I was listening to was a kind of audio version of the unwritten part of Stevenson's *Weir of Hermiston*.' 'Who was that extraordinary man with the notebook?' 'An afternoon nap is a way for old people to find a way of returning to their first state — that is, of the napping baby. The nap is the wellspring of life.' 'What really changed things for us was the discovery of a Martian meteorite in Antarctica. When we subjected it to geochemical analysis we discovered fossil traces of bacteria.' 'You interest me strangely.' I'm looking for Rupert. Where is the boy? He is never there when I want to apologise to him. We had a tiff and now our weekend is quite spoilt. I only wish to say I am sorry and kiss his cheek better.' 'That woman over there is like the carnivorous Venezuelan orchid aracamunia. Beautiful, but she devours men.' 'Levitations are a lot more common than one might think. For example, the nineteenth-century medium Daniel Dunglass Home not only levitated, but took a woman physician, Dr Harriet Clisby up with him. On another occasion, at Ashley Place in London, he floated out of one window and floated in the next.' 'So I thought I would round the evening off by going to a strip club. And, lo and behold, there was my psychoanalyst performing on stage and we clocked one another. Embarrassing? I'll say. But better than being in bed with a dead policeman.'

'Speaking of policemen, there are some coming our way now and two of them have guns. They also have dogs.'

It was true. Most people were being hurried by the police out of the grounds, though Marcus, Charles and Mortimer were frantically running around and selecting those whom they wished to have take shelter in the house. Tom was among this group.

'What's up?' Tom asked Sylvie who was running beside him.

'Apparently someone has seen a polar bear loose in the grounds.'

'No,' said Tom. 'That will be an escaped Siberian white

tiger called Snookins.'

'You are kidding.' Then Sylvie dropped back to let Lancelyn catch up.

They passed a police marksman who was on alert outside the door and they all made it in safely into the house. About twenty of them stood about in the hall nervously chatting and wondering how long it would take to sort this crisis out. After about half an hour Ferdie came in to report.

'Fucking Rupert! I can't tempt Snookins back into his cage. He is enjoying chasing and eating the peacocks too much. I have squared it with the police that Snookins will not be shot — not with bullets at least. A team is on the way from London Zoo and they will bring him down with tranquiliser pellets. Obviously this will take some time. Don't look at me like that. It's not my fault. It's bloody Rupert. He let Snookins out to make me sorry.'

Marcus was indeed looking thunderous. He produced a hip flask and took a big swig from it as he considered what should happen now. Then he looked at Charles who nodded.

'Nobody can leave the house, except for Ferdie,' said Marcus. 'Therefore I suggest that we bring forward the playing of the second tape of Edward Raven. This was to have been tomorrow morning, but now I think that those who are concerned should assemble in the library in half an hour's time.'

Half an hour later Lancelyn stood just outside the library. He was looking into the room and shuddering. It was plain that he was unable to make himself actually enter the room. Sylvie explained,

'He does not mind the odd thriller or whodunnit, but these

174

days he is afraid of libraries or of books in any quantity. I think he is scared of the stories that libraries may contain.'

Mortimer was reassuring, 'There is no need to worry about that. There are few if any stories in the library of Marcus Wainwright. Instead, it is the finest library devoted to coalmining in the country. Not even the library of the National Coal Mining Museum in Wakefield can match the collection that Marcus has assembled.'

Then Mortimer shoved him through the door.

CHAPTER EIGHTEEN

Those eventually seated at the long library table were Tom, Charles, Edward, Mortimer, Lancelyn, Sylvie, Bernard, Molly, Quentin, Marcus and Jaimie. 'Ferdie, whom most of you know as Mr Zamboni, will be joining us later'. Jaimie had been last to enter. His jaw was covered by an enormous bandage which was tied at the top of his head, so that he somewhat resembled a child with mumps. Mortimer grunted approvingly and jotted down something in his notebook. Molly looked at Jamie mournfully. Saffron, who had accompanied Jamie down to the library, was barred from entering by Marcus. She was not to be part of the oddly assorted group. Indeed she had not even been on Marcus' guest list for the reception.

Then Marcus, taking his seat at the head of the table, said,

'I expect you are all wondering why you are here.'

'Nope. Obviously there has been or will be a murder and we are all suspects,' said Quentin.

'And, one by one, the great detective will explore the motives and opportunities of all of us,' said Sylvie.

And Lancelyn chimed in with, 'But I expect the murderer will prove to be one of the policemen in the grounds. Or just possibly a man who claims to be a zoo keeper. Meanwhile we are cut off from the outside world.'

Marcus waved these frivolous suggestions away, 'What I propose is that we listen carefully to the tape and then we hold a discussion about its meaning and its personal consequences for us. Though I was thinking of something like a symposium, Molly and Ferdie thought that this discussion should have more the personal feel of an encounter group, something of which they have had experience, and I believe that Tom also has also been in an encounter group. Ferdie was suggesting that we all sat on the floor and took our clothes off, but I think we are a bit too old for that and a few of us might even have difficulty in getting back up off the floor. So you may remain in your seats. Now… Charles?'

Charles reached under the table for the old Grundig tape recorder and the tape which was still in its box. He showed them the box.

'Raven wrote on here the approximate date on which the tape should be played and he also provided a shortlist of some of the people who should be present at its playing. I am sure that we are all most grateful to Sir Marcus for facilitating our gathering and our learning what Raven's message is for us.'

Charles found it a fiddly business getting the end of recorded tape attached to the empty spool, but at last it was done.

'Let the wild rumpus begin,' muttered Sylvie.

What followed had the feeling of a séance and the voice of the dead man was faint and uncertain, 'Our life is no novel, but it should and could become one… no, that is not the right place to start. Let me start with me. Who was it who wrote of being "fastened to a dying animal"?'

TOM'S VERSION

'It was W. B. Yeats,' said Tom. The others swiftly hushed him.

Raven's voice continued, 'Whoever it was, that is my condition and, as I speak to you today, I am conscious of being in a race against my fading mental powers and against death itself. A race which I am bound to lose. Yet, though dead, I acquire an afterlife of a sort by being present in your stories and talking to you now. It is naturally impossible for me to visualise the circumstances in which you are listening to this, as well as the full complement of the audience and the locale. So many decades on, you should have the technology to show a three-dimensional image of me as I talk, but of course that technology was not available to me when I recorded this, and, for all I know, my audience is seated in a domed space colony on the Moon or Mars.

'By now some of you must be about as old as I was when I made this tape and your dancing days are over. It is now time for you to reflect back on the lives that you have led. Molly are you there? Still as glamorous as ever? I wish I could see you. You made me realise that feminine beauty could be... well, never mind. I especially wanted you to have a good life. The Ignatian exercises should lead to salvation. It has to be salvation or damnation. But I am getting ahead of myself... perhaps I am always ahead of myself.

'How are we held together? Of course, our skin stops our blood, water and other fluids from spilling out all over the place. But no. How are we held together psychically? I believe... no, I am certain that stories serve as our psychic skin and that we are held together by the stories which we tell about ourselves. We all tell these self-referential stories, but, when we consider the overwhelming mass of mankind, the stories they tell are banal in the extreme, repetitive, incoherent and they fail to reach any kind of climax before death puts a full stop to their stories. Such stories are the poorly shaped products of the common life, and they lack the quality of romance and, in words of one literary critic, they do not have "a halo of mystery, an atmosphere of strangeness and adventure". Now, I do not know how much you have discovered about my own strange career, but however good or bad my career was, I may fairly claim that it was mysterious.

'Bernard and Lancelyn (I hope you are there and listening to me), you may have wondered why I set you that final undergraduate essay on ghost stories, for, after all, it could be said that it started everything. Ghost stories are special in several ways. First, they demonstrate the power of the past and the fictional manifestation of a ghost is usually accompanied by a back story — a woman burned as a witch, children who had their hearts cut out, a man who in the past has consulted with the Devil in Chorazin — that kind of thing. Secondly, a story is something that is not real. Ghosts are not real. It follows that there is a double level of unreality in a ghost story. Thirdly, the best ghost stories challenge rationality in a subtle way, since the rational explanation for the ghostly manifestation will usually be less plausible than the supernatural one.'

At this point Ferdie entered and quietly took his seat. He was smiling.

'The quest for the story is the story — as in *Treasure Island*, in which the money is much less important than the adventure itself. But in your case — may I call you my disciples? — the quest for the *meaning* of your story is the *meaning* of your story. I fear I am not making myself clear and, across the decades, I sense puzzled looks. Let me try again and from a different direction. The filmmaker Pier Paolo Pasolini once remarked that "The truth does not reside in one story but in many stories". As in film and literature, so in life. The lives that some at least of you in my audience have been leading conform to a pattern, even though that pattern may not be detectable in one life or even two or three. If the right sort of pattern has been set up, then the people who are part of its structure will inhabit a flesh and blood romance which has been concealed within the humdrum ordinary world. Indeed, they must inhabit it. Escape is impossible. This may all sound rather mystical. It is intended to be mystical. *Ipso facto...*'

Lancelyn, who had his eyes closed, now opened them.

'Who is he calling fatso?'

He looked round the room before coming to a decision.

'It is probably Marcus,' he said, before closing his eyes again.

Raven's voice continued, 'I have been doing God's work, for God loves a good story. Besides people's lives are improved by being put in a story. So... oh dear, I wish I knew what I was trying to say. I guess I must try yet again. Molly, Bernard and Lancelyn, I envisaged a *Jules et Jim* relationship for the three of you, yet the precise nature of the story matters less than that there should be a story. My chosen ones, you are nearing the ends of your lives. More important, you are nearing the end of the story that I had engineered. The universe you live in has been generated by the patterns created by my mind, but you now need a new pattern and for that you need a new master patternmaker. Happily I did arrange for this... for this... I am afraid that I have momentarily forgotten the name. Never mind. Perhaps that person is sitting beside you. What I would hope for is a group of stories running in parallel about spiritual redemption. As I say, you are nearing the end of your lives...'

'Particularly the one who is going to get murdered,' muttered Quentin.

Raven's voice continued, 'Some of you may have the sense that your lives are unravelling. I think that I can assure you that it will all turn out well in the end... well, maybe not so sure... but now think of this. One wants to get to read to the end of a story and at the same time one does not want to get to the end of a story. One wants, because one wants to know how it ends. One does not want, because one does not want the pleasure of immersing oneself in a story to come to an end. Now there is a contrast between the story on the page and the story as lived, since, in almost all cases, the person who is living a story not only does not want to know how it will end, but he also has no wish at all for that end to be reached. So what follows... oh dear, they are coming for me...'

With that the voice ceased and there was the sound of furniture being moved about before the tape ended.

'Well, I will not conceal from you what is obvious,' said Charles. 'This is a disaster. All I can say is that you should have heard Raven in his prime. He was brilliant.' Charles was angry in his disappointment. 'We will shortly reconvene to discuss our responses to what we have heard and what sense we can make of it. I hope there will be some point to all of this.'

Now everyone was looking at Lancelyn who had suddenly begun to shudder, having just noticed a particular shelf of books. Sylvie tried to restrain him, but he leapt to his feet.

'Kobolds! I am not staying here,' and, as fast as he could, he hobbled out of the room, just occasionally pausing to brandish his stick as if it were a sword. Others now crowded round the shelf in question. Marcus explained, 'These books are devoted to the occult qualities of the mineral cobalt which derives its name, "goblin ore", from the kobolds, or spirits of the mines, who haunt the mines and plague the miners. The kobolds live and breathe in rocks. Their warning knocks presage disasters in the pits. Cobalt has long been thought to be an evil underground element.'

'After his illness, Lancelyn is afraid of weird books,' said Sylvie.

Ferdie was now able to report to Marcus, 'It is all under control now. Snookins is safe and sleeping in his cage. The police are hunting for Rupert. They want to charge him with something.'

Then Marcus conferred with a servant before telling those who were still in the library that the grand formal dinner followed by fireworks that had been planned was now off. Some of the staff who had been shepherded out of the grounds had not yet returned and things were at sixes and sevens. Instead a scratch buffet would be provided after the so-called encounter group. Marcus concluded by calling Tom over for a word.

'Tom, we want you to act as the meeting's leader or facilitator, or whatever the right word is.'

'Why me?'

'Neither I nor Charles has any experience of encounter groups. Then, as you may have noticed, Ferdie has gone a bit mad and Molly just has too much history. Besides Sylvie would walk out, taking Lancelyn with her if Molly was made group leader. You have encounter group experience and we want someone sane.'

Tom felt vaguely flattered and shrugged.

CHAPTER NINETEEN

Twenty minutes later he found himself sitting at the head of the table in the library and readying himself to call the meeting to order. Lancelyn had to be gently coaxed in and seated as far away from the kobolds as possible. Faced with another wall of sound, Tom had difficulty in getting people's attention.

'This is so bloody seventyish.' 'Raven has been playing with our lives.' 'Playing and losing.' 'I like the idea of us all being special people.' 'It is all Lombard Street to a china orange that he is gay.' 'Perhaps we can get some pillows from upstairs so that we can symbolically explore conflicting opinions with pillow fights.' 'Mustn't grumble.' 'I don't know what you are going to say since you were asleep during most of the tape.' 'I concentrate better with my eyes shut.' 'I don't think it will turn out to be an encounter group. It will probably be more like a symposium — the sort of thing Plato or Lowes Dickinson wrote about.' 'Who's he?' 'Philip Toynbee also wrote one called *Thanatos* in which nine characters discussed death'. 'I think we should do old age.' 'What is your favourite gas giant?' 'That has to be Saturn.' 'I wasn't expecting a fucking sermon'. 'I thought it was all a bit of an anti-climax.' 'But I hate climaxes.' 'I wish I could understand what this

Ignatianism was. Is it terribly fashionable?'

At length Tom was able to bring them to order. He explained that he was not their ringleader, but their facilitator. As Charles had already suggested, each person in turn should say a bit about themselves and what needed saying in the wake of Raven's tape. They should feel free to say whatever was on their mind, but no more than ten minutes please. He would be last to speak. Then turning to the person on his right, he suggested that Sylvie should speak first.

'OK. I'm nothing special. I never knew Raven and I still have no idea what Ignatianism is. Lancelyn cannot or will not explain it. All I have done is loved and cared for Lancelyn after he was so abominably abused, tortured and driven mad by that pair.'

And she pointed first at Molly and then at Jaimie.

Molly literally spat.

'You hideous shrew! That's not how it was, you cow. You know that it was not like that. We should…'

Tom cut her off, 'You will have your turn, Molly.'

Sylvie continued, 'Bugger encounter groups or symposiums. I think this should be a trial with these two in the dock as the accused and the rest of us serving as the judges and jury. Gentlemen of the jury, these two used cruel sex games to humiliate and destroy Lancelyn. He lost his teaching post, his great library and for a while his mind. As for Raven, if that was part of his great plan, then it was ridiculous and completely evil and mistaken. Nothing happened as he prophesied. I have seen *Jules et Jim* and it was not all like what happened to Lancelyn. And Jaimie! Oh Jaimie! By now I know you so well. A demon in a lecturer's gown. He lured me away from my first husband who then leapt to his death from a ruined cathedral tower. But not long after that Jaimie dumped me for this high-class Oxbridge slut. She has used her sex to destroy first Bernard and then Lancelyn and probably other men since.'

'Time for that pillow fight,' suggested Ferdie, while Lancelyn was muttering, 'Water under the bridge, dear. All water under the bridge.' But she ignored them both.

'Molly's sadism comes out in that ridiculous Russian novel she wrote with all that high-flown gloomy philosophy being bunged in as the prelude to yet another lubricious flogging with the rod or the knout. By the way, I must take this occasion to thank Mortimer for giving Jaimie just a little of what he deserved. Thank you, Mortimer. You are a brick. That's it. I think that I have run out of things to say.'

Now it was Bernard's turn.

'Can't we stop this right now? Unpleasant things, untrue things are bound to be said. Besides I am feeling peckish.'

'No, Bernard, it is your turn.'

So he continued, 'As most of you know, I was a student of Raven's and I was one of those who were privileged to be initiated into the Ignatian technique of meditation. It got me my starred first and then a research fellowship at All Souls. But, soon after that, I let Raven down and betrayed his hopes for me. I apostatised and went over to critical theory. Critical theory, so modern and so much the language of my colleagues and rivals in the academic study of literature, seemed to promise fresh approaches and penetrating verdicts on every text that might fall under its examination, whereas *The Spiritual Exercises of St Ignatius of Loyola* was just so very seventeenth century and apparently without any contemporary relevance. So I strayed and I think I was punished for it.

'Yet I have since returned to the fold and I have found that, not only is the intensity of the visualisation technique valuable for mapping the terrain of Mars, but the study of Mars in turn leads me on to the contemplation of eternal things and an approach to the Divine. What a miracle it is that we find ourselves on this Earth! All our assignations, dreams and strivings take place on a planet that is effectively a tiny Garden of Eden, while all around us and only a few miles up or down one enters a malevolent environment of winds, gases, flames and molten rock. Mars is a mass of rusting iron and the similar deadness of the other planets that accompany us in our circuit round the Sun are a commentary on the futility of human endeavour, as they seem to menace us with their indifference. In the rotation of the nine planets we can discern the nine circles of Hell. There is a horrid Dantesque poetry about the solar system: the cyclopean geology of Mars, Titan's seas of liquid methane, the steady drizzle of sulphur on Venus, centuries-old storms on Jupiter, mineral seas and metallic snows abounding elsewhere. Faced with such menacing grandeur, we know ourselves to be small and pitiful. Personally I have no fear of my own end, yet what I do fear is the death of the Sun. In five billion years' time it will begin to incandesce and long before then everything human will be damned and doomed. The impending death of the Sun and the following eternity of lifelessness terrify me. Um… as a young student of literature, I failed to understand that the truest poetry is not in Chaucer or Keats but in the structure and composition of the universe. Moreover, and this was shameful, the brotherhood of science was invisible to me. The scientists of the Bradbury Institute rescued me from myself. My one regret in life is that I have been born too early to have a hope of setting foot on Mars, for we are still at the early stages of drawing up the blueprints. Um... I suppose that all this is not very relevant to the tape we have been listening to. Since I do not have anything useful to say about that, I suppose that I should give way to my old friend Lancelyn.'

Lancelyn cleared his throat and began, 'When we were in Samoa...'

'Lancelyn, please not that yet again!' Sylvie was frantic.

'It is alright, dear. I was only going to say that whatever it was that we witnessed in Samoa made me realise that there are holes in the world which we inhabit and these holes allow the supernatural to seep through and manifest themselves. I think also of that time in Merton when Marcus, Bernard and I sat drinking vodka out of coronation mugs and for one brief instant I glimpsed the spirit of evil moving across my bookcase. Of course, only some people can see the supernatural and probably it is their misfortune, for I think that it is a weakness, a kind of illness even. It is a bit like being unusually prone to coincidences. People in novels are often prone to coincidences or to supernatural visitations. It may be that it is from some such weakness that I get my vague sense that I might be living in a novel. Perhaps the Ignatian technique carries a kind of contagion which allowed Raven to infect his chosen students with narratives. Perhaps repeated use of the Ignatian technique turns one into a character who seeks an author and then an adventure. I don't know... having asked that and similar questions, I have given up trying to answer them. I try not to think too much about anything. Besides, I can no longer do the

Ignatian exercises after electroconvulsive therapy destroyed my powers of concentration. As I was saying to someone earlier today, I have become an intellectual eunuch. These days I find myself increasingly returning in memory to my boyhood at Eton. Who was it who said "*Les vrais paradis sont les paradis qu'on a perdus*"?'

'Proust,' said Bernard.

'And Proust did not have the benefit of an Eton education! At Eton I experienced myself as an arrow being aimed up at the sky. I was young. I flexed my muscles. I hurried forward. I wished to learn so much. I gazed over landscapes full of opportunity. And I felt desire, a desire that was all the more exciting because I could not guess what it was that might be the object of my desire. Yet still I longed for this mystery. Now here I am, an old man who has been listening to another old man who was close to death and I ask myself why can we all not be friends as we approach the great darkness? We must love one another as we prepare to die. Let everyone forgive everyone.'

Then it was Mortimer's turn, 'Do I have to say something? If so, I have to say that I find this group-confessional business simply absurd — as cockamamie as a Nepalese clog dance. You lot are so many dead ringers for the unhappy members of a family who, having assembled in hope to hear the reading of the will of the deceased, have just learned that the deceased has left all his money to a charity that is devoted to the care of disabled mutts. I know that I am not the most popular person in the room — except now with Sylvie, and thanks, Sylvie, and you are welcome. Nobody should ever dare mess with a former student of Raven's. Some things are ineffable.

"Whereof we cannot speak thereof we must keep silent" and then, when words cannot serve, a good punch will usually do the job better.

'Glad to hear Lancelyn mention Proust. I yield to no one in my admiration for Proust's *Remembrance of Things Past* and in particular Proust's treatment of violence and war. "War is something that is lived like a love or a hatred and could be told like a novel". As Proust observed, on a battlefield, it can be hard to distinguish someone who is bringing succour to a wounded man from someone who is determined to finish the wounded man off, and that is what sexual cruelty is like. Then at the individual level one thinks of the gaze of pretty Albertine that is so obsessive and corrosive that it seems that it must tear the skin off the face that she is gazing at. Also there is that delicately evoked scene in which the Baron de Charlus is chained to a bed and whipped and there is also Jupien's egging on of the vicious gigolos. Desire and pain are forever chained together.

'The gimp got what was coming to him, but Molly I will never punch. She is after all a lady and besides Raven was fond of her, and beauty has its privileges. What is more, I like to think of myself as a chivalrous type. But, as for this whole set-up here, it is like a drawing-room comedy in which the joke is that none of the characters can find the drawing room. Over to you, Marcus.'

'Thank you, Mortimer. I am relieved to hear that you have no current plans to knock Molly's teeth out. Molly and I went to the same history lectures in Oxford. In those days I was very shy indeed. As soon as I encountered her, I thought that she was most marvellous thing in the world I had ever seen and I wanted her to become my girlfriend and then my wife. But fate threw her in the way of two more confident undergraduates, Bernard and Lancelyn, and that was that. These days, though I am so very grand in other peoples' eyes, I am just the same as I was when I was a student, terribly, terribly shy and nervous. I know I drink too much and I think that is why I drink so much. That is my excuse at least. I even need alcohol to give me the Dutch courage to go to bed and face the terrors of the night. Why do they make getting in or out of underpants so complicated? I also know that it is my wretched shyness that makes me so angry, so often. Now Molly is my chatelaine, my nursemaid, my goddess. I live in terror that she may leave me. I know that she cannot always be faithful. It is alright, Molly, I understand — at least I do when I am sober. I never met the famous Raven and am finding it difficult to understand what all the fuss was about. Still I know that he was very fond of Molly and that must count in his favour.

'On quite another matter, I was talking earlier today with Ferdie, though our conversation was cut off. This was just before the snow tiger escaped and he was checking with me about the night of the séance in St Andrews at which Lancelyn, Bernard, Molly, Quentin, myself and my former wife, Janet, were all present. This was many years ago. In the course of that abortive séance the letters taken randomly from a tin of alphabet spaghetti seemed to spell out a message of hatred to Lancelyn. Ferdie wanted to know if he was right in guessing that I had purchased the tin in Davenport's magic shop in the Charing Cross Underground Arcade. Yes, Ferdie, you were quite right. I did buy the ingeniously contrived tin there and my original plan was that on what would be the day after the séance, the letters would spell out HAPPY BIRTHDAY to one of Janet's children. The trick tin had cellophane dividers on which one could arrange the letters at will. So far so good, but once the oh so serious and sombre séance was under way and an assortment of letters was needed in order to receive some portentous message from the Other World, I went into the kitchen and fished out the letters on one of the tin's levels which would make an ominous message. It wasn't directed at Lancelyn particularly. I didn't know who would be receiving a helping of baleful spaghetti and it was all intended as a joke, especially as Lancelyn and Bernard were so sceptical about the supernatural. They thought that the supernatural was a social construct or something. But then everybody took the message of the letters so seriously that I dared not confess. It has been on my conscience ever since. Enough of that. To wind up, today has been a remarkably busy day, overstuffed with surprises, most of them unpleasant. Everything all at once. Someone once said that "Time is what stops everything happening at once".'

'I expect it was Quentin,' said Lancelyn. 'He often used to say things like that.'

'I don't remember doing so, Lancelyn, but I suppose I might have done,' said Quentin. 'If it can be my turn to speak now, I too never knew this man, Raven, but I am pretty sure that I have not missed much. I gather that he had a rather unsavoury past. What is more, he seems typical of a breed of literary critic, such as F.R. Leavis, Raymond Williams and Edward Said, who develop delusions of grandeur and come to believe that it is their destiny not only to diagnose the ills of society and culture, but also to take the lead in the manner of their reform. In my view Eng. Lit. academics should confine themselves to teaching boys and girls how to read good books properly. Raven's belief that he has turned my life and your lives into stories is plainly a manifestation of his megalomania, though perhaps we should feel compassion for an old man who was losing his marbles. In general, historians are much saner and, I think, nicer people.

'Even so, my story is a strange one. I have spent most of my life impersonating a historian of the Tudor age. About ten years ago this fraud culminated in my publication of *Pilgrimage of Blood*, a wide-ranging revisionist account of the Pilgrimage of Grace. That got me my professorship and a little later my emeritus status. Only then was I able to tear the Tudor mask from my face.

Only then was I able to research and write about the only period which truly interested me. In *An Autobiography and Other Essays* the historian G.M. Trevelyan wrote: "The poetry of history lies in the quasi miraculous fact that once, on this earth, once on this familiar spot of ground, walked other men and women, as actual as we are today, thinking their own thoughts, swayed by their own passions, but now all gone, one generation vanishing into another, gone as utterly as we ourselves shall shortly be gone, like ghosts at cockcrow." Yes, that is the true poetry and pathos of history. "We ourselves shall shortly be gone." I am a little older than most of you. You see a bald academic and logophiliac. But I know myself to be an aged hippy and in my imagination I have let my hair flow down to my shoulders.

'I have now set myself to my real task as a historian which is to chronicle sixties London as I knew it. The days of hope.

The Arts Lab, Gandalf's Garden. I Was Lord Kitchener's Valet. Bunjie's Coffee House and Folk Cellar. Dark They Were and Golden-Eyed. Better Books. I have become the chronicler of my youth and its lost enchantments. Julie and I and our friends all lived in this dream, so full of light, colour and love. I have come to think of it as a strangely disguised re-enactment of the ill-fated Children's Crusade of 1212. The trouble was that we knew it was a dream, for the songs of that time told us that this was so. The doom was spelt out in songs in which we heard youthful voices prophesying. We listened to The Beatles' *When I'm 64* and to Donovan's *Hi It's Been a Long Time* and to The Incredible String Band's *First Girl I Loved* and to Joni Mitchell's *Both Sides Now*. The songs told us that few years on, older and more resigned, one might reencounter one's first girlfriend and share the lament that we had lost the battle against real life. So it was. Quite suddenly The Arts Lab and Dark They Were and Golden-Eyed vanished and Julie was no longer at my side. We were due to meet as usual at the Chelsea Arts Club, but she never turned up. Despite the songs, I never re-encountered her. She had been a phantom of youthful desire dressed by Biba. I study photographs and old clips of sixties London scenes in the hope of catching a glimpse of Julie once more at my side — history as heartache. Soon I shall be a ghost at cockcrow and perhaps Julie has gone ahead of me.

'Now, on quite another matter, I think we should take a vote on who in this room is most likely to get murdered tonight. Then perhaps we could have a second vote on whom we would most like to see murdered. Then a third vote on who we guess the murderer will be.'

'We are not prepared to see the symposium, or encounter

group, or whatever it is turned into a balloon debate,' said Charles. 'Thank you, Quentin. It is my turn now. Some of you heard me speak briefly at Raven's funeral when I played his first tape. Since then I have been made aware of a number of things which are not to his credit, most obviously his paedophilia, his time in prison and his invention of his military service during the war. And yet... and yet, a sinner may repent and, having repented, the strength of his sense of his former sinfulness may compel him to do more good in the world than he would ever have previously dreamt that he or anybody else could be capable of. Like several of you here, I learned to use the Ignatian technique to enter books like *Robinson Crusoe* and *Great Expectations*. But then I thought that it might be better and closer to the intentions of St. Ignatius to use his recommended exercises in visualisation in order to enter the New Testament and walk with Christ, and for the past thirty years or so this is what I have done. I am a Christian soldier. I have served in Afghanistan, Iraq and Lebanon and in all these places and others there has always been a Bible in my knapsack, not only that, but the Bible is also within me at all times, so that I am able see the colour, passion, and violence of its narrative without even having to open my knapsack. I have seen Exodus, Lamentations, Maccabees and Revelations played out in the Indian subcontinent and the Middle East.

'So it is that I have been drawn closer to God. I want to tell you what a fearful things that is. In the course of my service in the U.S. armed forces plenty of shots have been fired at me. Yet I have found myself to be much less afraid of bullets than I am of Divine ecstasy. Ecstasy is a truly fearful thing. It hollows a man out. There is much pain in this Divinely dispensed pleasure. On each ecstatic occasion one has to die a little before God. The awareness of God peering into my soul and registering all my sins is shame and horror to me. The infinite and the eternal are fearful things. It is better not to think about them. Now shall I tell you what God is like? I shall not. Instead I shall tell you what Einstein said when he was asked by a reporter to explain relativity. This is the story he told: 'A man was asked by a blind man to describe the colour white. The man said, "White is the colour of a swan." "The blind man said, "What is a swan?" The man said, "The swan is a bird with a crooked neck." "The blind man asked, "What is crooked?" The man was becoming impatient. He grabbed the blind man's arm and straightened it and said, "This is straight." Then he bent it and said, "And this is crooked". Whereupon the blind man quickly said "Yes, yes. Thank you. Now I know what white is."' This symposium, for all its triviality and incoherence, seems to me to be a foretaste of the Final Judgement in which I shall be assessed, and those whom I have wronged will rise up against me, and I shall be found wanting. A parodic foretaste, but still a foretaste. My life is no more than a form of chrysalis from which I shall emerge into the afterlife. I wish I did not know these things. Raven taught me how to pray and I curse him for it.'

Charles looked to Ferdie who now spoke, 'Hey, lighten up man! The Quaesitor encounter group was much more touchy-feely and there were laughs along the way. None of this ultimate things stuff. What Marcus was saying about alcohol is sort of true for drugs and methedrine especially is alcohol squared. I owe everything to magic beans. Let me explain. My story is a strange one. I was a pimply youth, my girlfriend had just dumped me and I was expecting to soon start work in a milk bottling plant in Basingstoke, but I came up to London on what I believed to be one of my last days of freedom. But then by chance (but can it really have been chance?) I came across Davenport's magic shop in that subterranean passage by Charing Cross Station. You heard Marcus mention it. These days you read about the sixties and it is all bubble blowing, flowers in the hair and lots of grooving, but it wasn't really. I don't agree with Quentin on that. For the most part the sixties was very dingy, very dowdy. Except for the Davenport shop. Its colours blew my mind. I entered the shop walking as a sleepwalker walks. It was impossible to take it all in: Chinese and Indian robes, mannequins, wands, bunches of flowers, card packs, rubber eggs, interlocked silver hoops, posters of the great magicians, Chinese boxes, plastic skulls, ventriloquists' dummies, the headless lady and the doll's house of illusion. Such colours. Hitherto I had been living in the black and white world. Now I was somewhere else.

'I was confused and when the man at the counter asked what I was looking for, I told him that I wanted to buy some magic beans. I said "magic beans" for the sake of something to say. I really did not know what it was that I wanted from this marvellous shop. He looked puzzled and asked what did I want them for? In my desperation I told him that it was so that I could climb up the beanstalk and get ever so high right out of this world. The shopkeeper stroked his chin as he wondered how to respond to my request. But, standing beside me there was another customer, a sharp nosed man with wispy hair and he put his mouth to my ear and whispered that he could get me magic beans that would take me as high as I wanted. I just had to follow him out of the shop. Then having collected a large parcel from the man behind the counter, he dragged me out of the shop and up the steps to the pavement. Having hailed a taxi, he pulled me into it and the taxi delivered us to his flat, God knows where. I didn't know London in those days.

'The flat was nothing like any place that I had been used to. The walls were white but they carried extraordinary charcoal frescoes of cavorting nymphs, satyrs and hunting dogs. He put some loud music on the stereo. Diana Ross and the Supremes. Then he produced what he said were "magic beans". I looked at the small glass phials and said that they were not magic beans, but he said that this was modern packaging and they were magic. He broke open one of the phials and poured its liquid into a glass of white wine which he told me to drink. Then he mixed the same for himself. The stuff was just beginning to have an effect on me when a Catholic priest with bad breath entered. He too took a phial with a glass of wine. Then the wispy-haired man opened the parcel that he had picked up at the shop.

'What happened next was weird. He picked out something from the parcel and unwrapped it. He blew on this light bulb and then sent it into the air so that it floated just below the ceiling where it glowed on and off. Then he produced a trilby hat from the parcel and commanded me to watch as it danced on the table. Finally, having drained his glass of wine and methedrine — yes, the "magic beans were methedrine — he smashed the glass on the table and scooped up some of the larger fragments and chewed them. He stuck his tongue out for me to see that it was covered in small bits of glass before he finally swallowed them. The next thing that happened was that he and the priest stripped off and they buggered me. That was how I discovered sex, or rather sex discovered me. I was high and right out of this world. It seems to me that what I was experiencing then was very similar to the ecstatic experiences of Charles.'

Charles was scowling and shaking his head, but Ferdie continued, 'Yes, that first time the pain was exquisite, but it was just that, exquisite. There was beauty in its pain. I knew then that I was going to seek out more of the wonderful drug, that I would move heaven and earth to turn myself into a conjuror and that I was queer. Subsequently I was to find great comfort in something that the physicist J.B.S. Haldane once said, "The universe is not only queer. It is queerer than we can suppose".'

Now Bernard was objecting, 'Surely what you have just described was a series of hallucinations, whether drug-induced or not.'

'Oh no, the floating lightbulb and the dancing hat are standard in the conjuring repertoire. And, if someone will fetch a glass, I can guarantee to eat most of it.'

Marcus shook his head, 'No one should leave this room. But how were these tricks done?'

'I am sorry, but as a member of the Magic Circle I am sworn never to reveal how any trick is done. "*Indocilis privata loqui*", not apt to reveal secrets, is our motto. So there it is. "Magic beans" have made me who I am today, the great Zamboni! Bad for the teeth though. Looking back on the scene in the flat, I realise that the priest had meth mouth. One's mouth gets horribly dry on methedrine and the teeth start to erode. I love you all. That is the speed talking, but the speed speaks for me. I love Snookins, Rupert, Marcus and all of you here, even Mortimer who looks such a surly thug. I love you Mortimer.

Mortimer scowled. Ferdie continued, 'I also love me and I love the drug that makes me love. Wait till tomorrow when you will see me perform the operation of the transposed heads. You will be amazed.'

Marcus interposed, 'I am not sure that the conjuring is going to be on, Ferdie.'

'But it has to be. It will be the culmination of my career. One last thing. Does everyone here believe in fairies? Hands up those who believe in fairies.'

Only Tom and Bernard put up their hands, Bernard remarking as he did so, 'Einstein said "If you want your children to be intelligent read them fairy tales. If you want them to be more intelligent, then read them more fairy tales". Fairies open the gates of imagination.'

'I also believe in fairies,' said Ferdie, but that's nine fairies dead. I guess that you must be our next speaker, Molly.'

'Now we are going to hear her make an address to her various former lovers. This had better be good,' said Sylvie.

Molly responded, 'You all sound so fucking articulate — apart from that bitch Sylvie, that is. It is obvious to me that Sylvie does not love Lancelyn. She never has, but she does love his money. That is why she kept visiting him in that hospital in Dundee. She is a talentless, unproductive social parasite... but I am getting away from what I am wanting to express. You men seem to know what you want to say. Perhaps this is because you all know who you are. Sod that. I am an almost complete mystery to myself.

'I used to have regular lunches with Raven. He liked

to hear how Bernard was getting on and more generally he liked to get what Oxford gossip I could give him... he wanted Bernard and Lancelyn to leave academic life and eventually he was successful. But... um... I wonder about this Ignatian technique that some of you have been talking about and I wonder about Raven and whether he really understood what a novel is. Whereas I may not understand who or what I am, but I do understand novels because I write them. The only way fully to understand what is a novel is to write it. And, as I speak, I am beginning to wonder if it is not the case that I do after all know who I am because I am made by my writing. My identity is just that. Maybe that is mad, but perhaps it can be true for me. So when I created Natasha in *The Rod and the Knout* I also gave birth to me.

'Now for my "various former lovers". Yes. I am accursed and the malediction does not abate with the years. Indeed, now that I am so old, my lust seems to have more energy than I have and it drives me into men's beds whether I will or no. Can it really be evil to love men? I don't see why. At least I am someone. Yes, I know I am contradicting myself. I have made myself become someone — unlike that sodding parasitic witch over there. Nowadays I often think back to my childhood. I remember how pleasant it was, when I was a little girl, not to know about sex. In retrospect the enormous adult conspiracy to keep sex a secret from me seems quite charming. Eventually I did learn that there was no such person as Father Christmas, but in compensation there was sex. I research my novels in bed. By the way, my current one is about Semiramis, the sorceress queen of Babylon. I can do Semiramis, but beddable men provide the rest of the material I need. So the bed is a laboratory, in which lust and science have become partners. But Marcus, love, I will never leave you. Don't let me.'

Watching Molly speak, Tom had been wondering if there was there anything objective about a woman's beauty. If a chaffinch or a beaver looked at Molly would they recognise that she was beautiful?

She now gestured to Edward who sighed heavily before speaking, 'I guess some of you may be thinking that I am a dull dog who has spent most of his life totting up figures in a German bank and the rest of my time watering plants in my conservatory and it is true that I have spent much of my time doing something like that. Nevertheless I like to think that I have led a rather adventurous life with my orchids. You see I was successful in wangling extensive periods of leave, periods which I spent hunting for rare plants in Brazil, Columbia and the Philippines. Twice I have faced off tigers. I suffered a whole range of fevers. I have come close to dying from a poisoned dart. I had to fight for my life against another orchid hunter. Naturally I travelled heavily armed. Back in Europe, I also supplemented my very substantial German salary with a second fortune derived from my sale of the rarest orchids. And I have seen tropical sunsets, palms bending in monsoon rains, sapphire blue seas and long-haired maidens who danced just for me — and tribesmen who fed orchids with human blood. And, yes, it is the dangerous quest for the rare orchid that, in my eyes, gives that plant its true value and my greenhouse is a collection of personal adventures or stories. Not all my "adventures" can be classified as deeds of derring-do. Some of them are amorous, for I am yet another fan of Proust and taking my lead from his *Swann's Way*, I have become accustomed to use the arrangement of a cattleya orchid on a woman's bodice as a prelude to erotic fondling and, indeed "cattleya" has become code for sex in many of my relationships with women. So it is with Proust. "And long afterwards, when the rearrangement (or, rather, the ritual pretence of a rearrangement) had quite fallen into desuetude, the metaphor 'Do a cattleya,' transmuted into a simple verb which they would employ without thinking when they wished to refer to the act of physical possession…" It is hard for me to think of orchids without thinking of sex and danger. So I think that Raven was essentially right. But I now ask myself who is going to take over masterminding our adventures? Furthermore, what I want to know is, if I am a story, who is it who is reading me? Jaimie, can you answer that? It is your turn.'

'No. No idea about who is reading us,' said Jaimie and then gulped before continuing, 'For me the big question is why am I here? Everybody in this room hates me… well, just possibly not Molly. I don't know about her. Always a mystery. Anyway, the rest of you hate me. Despite Ferdie's words about loving everybody, I cannot believe that his "everybody" includes me. What is more everybody hates me with good reason. Quite some years ago I published an academic study, *The Problem of Evil in the Scottish Novel*. Though it was respectfully received, I felt dissatisfied with it. Something was missing. Slowly it came to me that my book was too bookish. In order to properly understand the evil of such characters as the Master of Ballantrae, Long John Silver and Mr Hyde, I had to become evil myself. I had to know what it was like to be hated and feared. Moreover, like Mr Hyde, I had to take on some kind of deformity, however vaguely defined, so that I became "evil made visible" with "Satan's signature upon me".

'This was difficult. There was no handbook, *Teach Yourself to Become Evil*.

Though I wanted to be evil, I was also cowardly. So I started small and groped my way forward. I started stealing things first from the department and then from shops. I began to treat Saffron as my slave. I deliberately bumped into old people in the street. I wrote to Janet and succeeded in breaking up Marcus' marriage to her and I stalked Molly. But this was all rather pathetic and was getting me nowhere. So then at last I took the big step forward and I murdered someone.'

Jaimie paused for dramatic effect and there were cries of 'Who?' and 'Why?' He then continued, 'I am not saying whom I killed or how I killed my victim, or where or when. Only that my victim was someone I did not know and who had no connection with me. That and there was a lot of screaming. I just needed a murder under my belt.'

'Aha! At last the perfect murder!' exclaimed Quentin. 'Better than I had hoped for.'

'I can beat it out of him,' growled Mortimer.

'It's a bluff,' said Bernard. 'He's a sicko.'

'Damnation is a fearful thing, James,' said Charles.

'Snookins can have him for breakfast,' said Ferdie.

Jaimie continued, 'With that deed I had made myself a free man. Now I knew for certain what it was like to be truly evil. Now I could read and fully understand such books as *Dr Jekyll and Mr Hyde*, *The Picture of Dorian Gray* and *The Talented Mr Ripley*.

I wonder about Raven. I wish I had got to meet him. Was he as evil as me? I also wonder what is Mortimer for? He is holding something back. I am sure of it. One more thing. I have noticed that since I have taken on the mantle of evil my beloved Scottish landscape has become malformed around me. The moorlands are now as bleak as any lunar landscape and the banks and braes, once so bonny, now tiresomely obstruct my passage through the wilderness. The mountains in their height menace me. Another thing, it has to be said that, looking round this room, I do not feel as out of place as I might have done when I was younger, for we all, or almost all, have become monsters in our old age, ugly creatures, smelly, hideously demanding, unpredictable in our actions and prone to temper tantrums. Yet you are looking at me as I were the only monster in the library. Something bad is going to happen while we are all here. I feel it in my bones and I look forward to it.'

Tom had found it increasingly difficult to concentrate on what was being said. It was like being in a queue to do a party improvisation and he was frantically trying to work out what he should say when it was finally his turn. Having watched Jaimie hurry out of the room, it was now Tom's turn, 'King Log thanks you. He would like to thank our speakers for making his job an easy one and for keeping well within the proposed time limits. As for what I can say, I do not know why I am here. I want to go home. I want to go back to Cashel, though it seems so far away. Listening to so many pointlessly competitive assertions of personal identity made me think of a Butlins seaside knobbly knees competition. Also, looking round the room, you are all so successful, Marcus the television magnate, Ferdie the Grand Zamboni, Molly the novelist and so on, whereas I am just a retired supermarket stock manager.

So I don't know what to say and anyway I usually find that W. B. Yeats has done my thinking and feeling for me. So let him speak for me now with his "Lines Written in Dejection":

"When have I last looked on
The round green eyes and the long wavering bodies
Of the dark leopards of the moon?
All the wild witches, those most noble ladies,
For all their broomsticks and their tears,
Their angry tears, are gone.
The holy centaurs of the hills are vanished;
I have nothing but the embittered sun;
Banished heroic mother moon and vanished,
And now I have come to fifty years
I must endure the timid sun."

You are not human beings. It seems that you have no parents and you have no children. If you have friends and neighbours. you do not talk about them. If you have work problems, you do not mention them either. Molly, what has your novel in progress about Semiramis got to do with anything? Why can you not write about people who are getting on with one another and struggling to make a living? Why can none of you accommodate yourselves to the necessary compromises of daily life? "You are nothing but a pack of cards!" I now declare this colloquy of monsters closed.'

'Does he really treat Saffron as a slave?' 'Tommy Cooper is my hero. I learned a lot from him.' 'An angry publisher gave me this scar.' 'Agathokakological means composed of both good and evil, but, as far as I know, there is no word for love of evil.' 'Not a peacock. The peacocks are all dead. That was the cry of a banshee.' 'Yes, he was so handsome, but there should be more to a man than good looks and brains and money.' 'Why are there no cavemen ghosts? Do ghosts have a restricted afterlife?' 'To quote, Yeats again, "Bodily decrepitude is wisdom; young we loved each other and were ignorant.' 'My mid-life crisis has come upon me rather late in the day.' 'If Raven were still alive, he would be able to point us in the right direction.' 'If my aunt had had balls, she would be my uncle.' 'In the end I decided that I was my own muse.' 'Bugger the death of the Sun. It's constipation that I worry about.' 'I used to be constipated until Janet divorced me.' 'I have never met a really evil person before. Will we be safe in our beds tonight?' 'Britain is no country for old men.'

After the group meeting, Sylvie announced that she and Lancelyn were not going to hang around to listen to more insults from Molly and they were leaving immediately for Cowes. Jaimie and Saffron were nowhere to be seen. The rest of the group had moved into the dining room where the noise of their chatter had seemed to rise and mingle with the smells of the food that had been laid out. Mortimer and Marcus were in close conversation. (What indeed *was* Mortimer for?) Ferdie, who was looking exceedingly cheerful, was surreptitiously stuffing his pockets with quails' eggs and sandwiches and he winked at Tom as he did so. Nobody wanted to talk to Tom after his closing speech. Moreover now that he was so old, he was beginning to suffer from ambient deafness and consequently he found it difficult to follow conversations in crowded rooms. So after a while he took his drink out onto the lawn and stood looking up at the stars. He heard shouting coming from indoors. Male voices were raised and there was obviously a terrible row going on inside. He decided not to go and investigate. Tomorrow transport would be arranged and he could return to Cashel. Almost an hour passed before he judged it safe to return indoors and find his way to his bedroom. He was very tired.

It was a night of strange noises and movements in the big house. Tom sat in a chair in the corner of the bedroom and listened for a while before taking his shoes off. Then he fell asleep.

'Wake up.'

He did so and he found that there was the barrel of a shotgun inches away from his head.

'Now stand up and strip,' commanded Molly.

He shook his head groggily. He was too old for this. Besides he did not want to betray Erin.

'Stand up and strip,' repeated Molly. 'In order to give our night together, which will probably be our last, more of an edge, I loaded the gun. This is not a joke gun.'

So he stripped and obeyed the commands that followed. The sex was not very satisfactory. It rarely was these days. Only when it was his turn to take the gun did Molly say something more, 'You missed something in the dining room. The reason that Mortimer did not punch me in the mouth today was that, as he so charmingly explained to me this afternoon, he was looking forward to me performing fellatio on him tonight and he did not want my appearance spoilt for this treat. He also told me that he was going to slip Marcus a Mickey Finn this evening, so that my absence from his bed would not be noticed later. I told him that this would not be necessary since Marcus regularly drank enough to pass out without any additional assistance from a drug, but Mortimer would not listen. So then at the buffet I saw him drop a pill into the gin that was in Marcus' hand. The trouble was that Quentin saw this too and decided that Mortimer was trying to poison Marcus. So he rushed forward and attempted to take the glass from Marcus. Whereupon Marcus became really furious, because he thought that Quentin was trying to stop him drinking so much. So he shoved him away and drained the glass, proclaiming as he did so that he was master in his own house and he would drink himself to extinction if he felt like it. Then Quentin made a grab for the glass which smashed to pieces on the floor. Quentin asked the butler to collect up all the bits, but Marcus decreed that the butler should see him to his bedroom as he had had enough of this day. Whereupon Quentin went down on his hands and knees and collected in a serviette as much of the glass as he could, presumably to be used in some future murder inquest. Meanwhile Mortimer was giving me significant looks. He will be in his bed waiting for me now. It will be a very long wait. Hell will freeze over. I thought that it would be more fun to be with you for old times' sake. You seemed so sad in the library and you seem sad now. Don't be sad. For old times' sake, I slipped down to the gunroom in the basement and fetched out one of the hunting rifles from their glass cabinet. Now I am yours to command. Don't worry about next door. Ferdie and Rupert got going earlier.'

She left his room as dawn was breaking.

CHAPTER TWENTY

Belatedly Tom remembered to take his pills with the breakfast orange juice. There were so many of them and with such exotic names. It was like a roll call of the lieutenants of Lucifer in Pandemonium. He was wishing that one of these demonic little pills might be an antidepressant and he was wondering if it would be easy, or even possible to return to Erin after what had happened last night.

Then he heard Quentin cry out, 'My God! He's alive!'

Marcus had entered the dining room, followed by Molly, and Marcus spoke, 'Could I have your attention please? For obvious reasons it was not possible to hold the conjuring session yesterday. But there will be a short magical performance in the marquee at eleven this morning. I had suggested scrapping the whole thing, but Ferdie is adamant. You are apparently going to see something that will be out of this world. This will be a sort of dress rehearsal for a Royal Command Performance later in the year. Ferdie also wanted to have the snow tiger on stage, but I am not having that. Nevertheless Ferdie has told me that his final act tomorrow will be a feat, never performed before, known as the "The Transposed Heads". It is not to be missed. After that Molly and I will see you on your various ways. I think that you will agree that it has been a memorable, if challenging, couple of days.'

Molly was elegant in an ivory white dress. She came over to Tom and said, 'When you have finished your breakfast, Ferdie wants to see us outside.'

They found Ferdie struggling to shoot up in the marquee. A leather strap was tight on his upper arm and he made a test squirt of the needle before tentatively moving it up and down over the arm.

He gave them a ghastly grin.

'Good morning. I used to just the drink the stuff, but you get a better, faster hit with the needle. By now it's getting damn hard to find a vein. Wait a bit and then I can tell you what I have in mind.'

They watched him essay several false starts with the needle, before it found a suitable vein and then he gave long shuddering sigh before turning to address them.

'I have a short standard repertoire of tricks to use as a warm-up. But for the climax of the Transposed Heads I shall need volunteers from the audience. You can help me out here by pretending to be slightly reluctant volunteers. Whereupon Naomi, my stage assistant will lead you to the cabinets over there at far end of the tent. Come with me.'

He led them to the two large crimson cabinets which were placed next to one another and decorated with chinoiserie cloud forms, pagodas, dragons and lotuses.

'These are the two cabinets which you are going to occupy. As you can see, each has a hole near the top and that is so your faces will be visible to the audience at all times. Also the upper section of the cabinet can and will be detached from the rest and the audience will see me insert these large metal blades into the two cabinets, so that the upper sections become clearly separated from the rest and then I will swap the two upper sections around so that Tom's head will seem to be resting on Molly's body and Molly's on Tom's. At least that is what they think they have seen. It will be good if you can both give big smiles at that point. Finally, I will open the cabinets to reveal that somehow your heads have after all remained attached to your respective bodies. You will find that the boxes are larger on the inside than they appear from the outside. The paintwork is deceptive in that way. When at the climax of the act I shout "Shazam Kabam!" you simply take one step back. There is nothing for you to worry about since I do all the work. It will all be tickety-boo. It is a variation on Robert Harbin's famous trick, the Zig Zag Girl. Got that? Is it all clear?'

This was all spoken at Ferdie's machine-gun speed.

'But how is it done?' Molly wanted to know.

'You know that I am a member of the Magic Circle. I am not allowed to tell you.'

'Fuck that. Fucked if I can see how this is going to work.'

So, though it was not clear at all, Molly and Tom left the tent. Using his stick, Tom cautiously lowered himself down onto the grass and sat in the Sun which was beginning to burn through the mist and he tried to imagine what it would be like to really find his head attached to Molly's softly voluptuous body. Then what would it be like to re-experience the full heat of sexual desire in the way that Molly apparently still did? If only Ferdie had the real magical power to give Tom a younger body. If my aunt had had balls...

When young Tom had wanted to be a poet. Looking back

on his youthful ambition, he now realised that his problem
had been just that. He had wanted to be a poet, but he did not
actually want to write poetry. He had had nothing poetic to say.
There was nothing poetic about him. Mortimer was right. He
was not even any good at rhyming. He did not even read much
poetry apart from Yeats. Whereas Molly really was a novelist,
even if she was a bad one. She lived her ridiculous stories.
These and similar gloomy reflections helped pass an hour.

> *'Cast a cold eye*
> *On life, on death.*
> *Horseman, pass by!'*

Then servants appeared and bustled about arranging benches
in the marquee. Some servants and a couple of gardeners
would also swell the audience of house guests. Ferdie, who
had changed, now appeared in his dinner jacket and turban
and he was followed by Naomi, the stage assistant. He did not
even wait for everybody to be seated before he started doing
card tricks, but he was doing them so fast that it was hard to
tell wherein lay the trickery. Then he produced a light bulb
and blew on it so that it floated up to the top of the tent where
it glowed on and off in just the way he had described on the
previous day. There was something perfunctory about all this.
Then he announced that he could read minds and he pointed at
Marcus, 'You sir, I can tell what you are thinking.'

'What am I thinking?'

'You are thinking that I cannot read your mind. Boom!
Boom! But now it is time to be serious. It is time to put away
card tricks and ingenious gadgets. Now it is time for you to

witness something that is truly magical. You will behold a woman with a man's head and a man with a woman's head, for this is the conjuration of the Transposed Heads. Though it has been attempted once before in Germany in the 1930s the outcome of that operation is not known for certain. Success in this conjuration today will serve as proof that the universe is not quite as rationally ordered as you think it is and that there are many marvels yet to be discovered. Now I need two volunteers from the audience, one male and one female.'

Molly and Tom slowly raised their arms and allowed Naomi to lead them up to Ferdie who stood in front of the cabinets.

'I think this is going to be a bit like a hemicorporectomy,' said Quentin.

'Can I have absolute quiet please?'

Ferdie ushered Tom and Molly into their respective cabinets and closed the doors. Then he stepped aside and made some mysterious passes with his hands before shouting 'Shazam Kabam!' and then thrusting metal plates through the upper sections of the cabinets.

POSTSCRIPT

Mortimer here. You, my mysterious reader, have got used to seeing everything through Tom's eyes. Like an attentive parrot, you have watched and listened to everything as from a vantage point on his shoulder. Not only that, but you have been allowed to read his thoughts and vicariously share his passions. At least that is what you thought your reading experience was, if you thought about it at all. But obviously this is no longer possible, since Tom was decapitated. His head lay at Molly's feet and her elegant ivory white dress was covered with his blood. It is time for me to step out of the shadows.

I guess that many of you were rooting for Tom and hoping that he would get back safely to Erin. Readers have a tendency to be taken captive by the narrative perspective. I myself rooted for the would-be assassin in Frederick Forsyth's *The Day of the Jackal*.

I admit that I am bitter that Molly did not come to my bed that night and chose to favour Tom instead. But I am not such a villain as to wish upon those two what happened to them in that marquee. Indeed I am not a villain at all. Did you really think a dud like Tom was up to the control of this narrative and the level of perception evident in the forgoing text? No dice. Forget about the telepathic parrot. If you think about it, I am a much more plausible narrator, since I was educated at Oxford, schooled in the Ignatian method and acquired further literary skills during my years as fiction editor of *The Times Literary Supplement*. Admittedly the text I have produced is anomalous. Although I have aimed at non-fiction (and in doing so I might add that I have been unsparing in my self-presentation) I did not directly witness all the scenes I have described and therefore at those points I have resorted to the licence of the novelist and conjured up the truth of those scenes as best I could.

After the Grand Guignol denouement of the Great Zamboni's final performance, things became rather tedious. Ferdie was arrested, tried and sentenced to six years in prison. This was despite considerable reason to suspect that Tom had chosen this dramatic way of committing suicide and that was indeed the case put forward by Ferdie's defending counsel. As for Molly and Marcus, I shall be looking after them. As time passes, the baggage of the years gets increasingly heavy.

I cannot think how many years have passed since my last meeting with Edward Raven. I happened to be in Oxford for a conference on the Celtic Twilight in literature and I was due to write a report on it for the *TLS*. Then I got a message from the organiser of the conference that Raven wanted to see me urgently. I skipped one of the duller papers and went over to Merton to find out what my revered former teacher could possibly need from me. He had aged a lot since I had last seen him. His plume of hair and his tuft of a beard were entirely white. Yet the ferocity of his gaze made me think of him as a young man trapped in an old man's body. After a glass of sherry and a few perfunctory enquiries about my work and the conference, he told me what he wanted me to do. The first was to post the two tapes by registered mail to Charles at the Pentagon. These tapes were in a sense his last will and testament, though quite some time must pass before the first should be played. The other thing was that he was appointing me his heir and he hoped that I would accept that. Though he had nothing of significant material value to leave, he wished to bequeath his grand project to me.

"You are my chosen one. You have the necessary strength and intelligence.

The tapes you are going to take away should keep our adventure on track.

But after the second tape has been played, it will be up to you to make any necessary adjustments that you think necessary to keep the story going."

Seeing me look uncertain, he added, "Things will be clearer when you have heard the tapes."

I wish this was the case, for I cannot believe that this was the end of the story that Raven was aiming for. It is bizarre to think back and recall that when I started this book it was to have been a celebration of the life and achievements of Edward Raven. Instead I present you with what looks like a study in multiple failures. But what I have now produced is not primarily that, for, as you can see, I have grafted it onto the earlier project which my great, if flawed, teacher entrusted to me, to continue the story that he envisaged and, if it should have strayed from that, then to correct its course and bring it closer to what he predicted and what the tapes expanded upon. It has been my duty to serve a mystery.

Why have I shown myself to be so horrible? Just for the hell of it? I knew that Tom's perception of me, or rather my presentation of Tom's perception of me was unflattering. But I also knew it was my duty to register what would obviously have been his feelings about me. It was hard to work with a character like that. He did not have a clue about Yeats, by the way. But I did my best to reconstruct his life and thoughts from our meetings and from what I have been told by Molly and others. I do not think that I am really a thug. I read Proust and Rilke and I am sad when I realise there is no room for someone like me in a novel by Proust or a poem by Rilke. As I worked on the narrative that you have before you, I sometimes had the uneasy feeling that, just as I wrote up Molly, Tom, Ferdie and the rest of them, so someone else might write me up. So be it. I am, like those I have written about, a prisoner of literature. My own book will never be published. Raven did not believe in publication and neither do I. There are enough novels out there already. I am my only reader. There is one last scene which has not yet happened and at which I will not be present, though I can easily imagine it…

Lancelyn put down the strange book he had been reading. He was waiting for Sylvie to come up on deck with the drinks.

THE END

RECOMMENDED READING

If you have enjoyed reading *Tom's Version* you have probably read its predecessor *The Runes Have Been Cast* and should also read Robert Irwin's other novels, particularly *Exquisite Corpse* and *Satan Wants Me*.

An author you should consider if you have enjoyed the novels of Robert Irwin is Andrew Crumey, and we recommend:

Pfitz
The Secret Knowledge
Beethoven's Assassins
Mobius Dick
Sputnik Caledonia

If you like clever unusual novels, we suggest you read:

Jabberwock by Dara Kavanagh
The Architect of Ruins by Herbert Rosendorfer
Before and During by Vladimir Sharov
New Finnish Grammar by Diego Marani
The Book of Nights by Sylvie Germain
Mr Dick or The Tenth Book by Jean-Pierre Ohl
The Prussian Bride by Yuri Buida
The Mussolini Canal by Antonio Pennacchi
The History of a Vendetta by Yoryis Yatromanolakis

For further info about our titles please visit www.dedalusbooks.com or email info@dedalusbooks.com for a catalogue.

Exquisite Corpse by Robert Irwin

'Robert Irwin's spectacular intense novel of love and madness among the provincial British surrealist movement works all the better because authentic factual detail is woven so effectively into the fancy.'   Roz Kaveney in *The New Statesman*

'The final chapter of the novel reads like a realistic epilogue to the book, but may instead be a hypnogogic illusion, which in turn casts doubt on many other events in the novel. Is Caroline merely a typist from Putney or the very vampire of Surrealism? It's for the reader to decide.'

Steven Moore in *The Washington Post*

'Robert Irwin is a master of the surreal imagination. Historical figures such as Aleister Crowley and Paul Eluard vie with fictional characters in an extended surrealist game, which, like the movement itself, is full of astonishing insights and hilarious pretensions. Superb.'

Ian Critchley in *The Sunday Times*

'*Exquisite Corpse* is one of the best novels I have read by an English person in my reading time. When I first read it I was completely bowled over.'

A. S. Byatt on *Radio 4's Saturday Review*

£8.99   ISBN 978 1 907650 54 3   249p   B. Format

Satan Wants Me by Robert Irwin

'Irwin is a writer of immense subtlety and craftmanship, and offers us a vivid and utterly convincing portrait of life on the loopier fringes of the Sixties. *Satan Wants Me* is black, compulsive and very, very funny.'

Christopher Hart in *The Daily Telegraph*

'Part of the book's fertile comedy stems from the ironic interweaving of the jargons of sociology, hippiedom and magick. It is hard to resist a pot-head mystic who hopes the Apocalypse will come on Wednesday because it will break up the week.'   Tom Deveson in *The Sunday Times*

'Robert Irwin's *Satan Wants Me* was a mad confection of black magic and 60s sexual liberation, a paranoid fantasy that drew heavily on the legacy of Aleister Crowley, but achieved a wonderful lightness of touch.'

Alex Clark in *The Guardian's Books of the Year*

'Pulsing with lurid detail and swarming with perverse characters — Aleister Crowley, Rimbaud and Janis Joplin all flit past — Irwin's erudite, sabre-sharp novel closes the gap between psychedelia and psychosis. A bad trip but a great journey.'   Victoria Segal in *The Times*

£9.99   ISBN 978 1 912868 20 9   320p   B. Format

The Arabian Nightmare by Robert Irwin

'Robert Irwin is indeed particularly brilliant. He takes the story-within-a-story technique of the Arab storyteller a stage further, so that a tangle of dreams and imaginings becomes part of the narrative fabric. The prose is discriminating and, beauty of all beauties, the book is constantly entertaining.'

Hilary Bailey in *The Guardian*

'...a classic orientalist fantasy tells the story of Balian of Norwich and his misadventures in a labyrinthine Cairo at the time of the Mamelukes. Steamy, exotic and ingenious, it is a boxes-within-boxes tale featuring such characters as Yoll, the Storyteller, Fatima the Deathly and the Father of Cats. It is a compelling meditation on reality and illusion, as well as on Arabian Nights-style storytelling. At its elusive centre lies the affliction of the Arabian Nightmare: a dream of infinite suffering that can never be remembered on waking, and might almost have happened to somebody else.'

Phil Baker in *The Sunday Times*

'Robert Irwin's novel *The Arabian Nightmare* was one of my favourite books of the early 1980s and one of the finest fantasies of the last century.'

Neil Gaiman in *Authors at Christmas*

'Robert Irwin writes beautifully and is dauntingly clever but the stunning thing about him is his originality. Robert Irwin's work, while rendered in the strictest, simplest and most elegant prose, defies definition. All that can be said is that it is a bit like a mingling of *The Thousand and One Nights* and *The Name of the Rose*. It is also magical, bizarre and frightening.'

Ruth Rendell

£9.99   ISBN 978 1 912868 62 9   266p   B. Format